Marie de Gentelles

The month of March

St. Joseph, protector of the Church, and model of Christians

Marie de Gentelles

The month of March
St. Joseph, protector of the Church, and model of Christians

ISBN/EAN: 9783741195969

Manufactured in Europe, USA, Canada, Australia, Japa

Cover: Foto ©Andreas Hilbeck / pixelio.de

Manufactured and distributed by brebook publishing software
(www.brebook.com)

Marie de Gentelles

The month of March

THE MONTH OF MARCH.

𝕴𝖒𝖕𝖗𝖎𝖒𝖆𝖙𝖚𝖗.

✠ HENRICUS EDUARDUS,
Archiepus Weſtmon.

23tia die Feb. 1872.

MONTH OF MARCH.

ST. JOSEPH,

PROTECTOR OF THE CHURCH, AND MODEL OF CHRISTIANS.

BY

MADAME DE GENTELLES,

AUTHOR OF 'APPEAL TO YOUNG CHRISTIAN WOMEN,' ETC.

TRANSLATED BY LADY HERBERT,

LONDON:

BURNS, OATES, AND COMPANY,

17, 18 Portman Street & 63 Paternoster Row.

Dedicated

TO

THE MEMBERS OF THE ASSOCIATIONS OF

'THE UNION OF CHRISTIAN WOMEN;'

TO THE 'CHRISTIAN MOTHERS;' AND TO THE

'CHILDREN OF MARY.'

Approval of the Bishop of Bayeux.

MADAME,—I have just read your *Month of St. Joseph*. I have found in it that which is so often wanting in books of this kind : I mean, a spirit of true and earnest piety. I hope it may do all the good which you hoped it would do when you proposed to write it.

Believe me, &c.

FLAVIEN,
Bishop of Bayeux and Lisieux.

Bayeux, 14th Feb. 1872.

To MADAME DE GENTELLES.

CONTENTS.

PONTIFICAL DECREE ASSIGNING ST. JOSEPH PATRON OF THE UNIVERSAL CHURCH.

DECRET. URBI ET ORBI.

IN the same way that God established Joseph, son of the Patriarch Jacob, Governor of all the land of Egypt, to insure to the people the necessary means of subsistence, so when the times were fulfilled for the Eternal Father to send His only Son to redeem the world, He chose another Joseph, of whom the first was the type; He made him lord and master of His house and His goods, and elected him as guardian of His principal treasures. And Joseph was espoused to the Immaculate Virgin Mary, from whom, by the power of the Holy Ghost, was born our Lord Jesus Christ, who deigned to be reputed the son of Joseph, and was subject unto him. And He whom so many kings and prophets had desired to see, Joseph not only beheld, but conversed with Him, held Him in his arms with paternal af-

fection, covered Him with kisses, watchéd
with care over His maintenance, and provided
for the nurture of Him who was to be the
spiritual nourishment of His faithful people,
and the Bread of eternal life.

In consequence of this sublime dignity conferred by God on His most faithful servant,
the Church has always held the blessed Joseph in the highest honour, after the most
Holy Virgin, his Spouse; has overwhelmed
him with praises, and has had recourse to
him, by preference, in her greatest distresses.
And as in these sad days the Church finds
herself assailed on all sides by her enemies,
and oppressed by such misfortunes that the
impious are persuaded that the time is come
when the gates of hell shall prevail against
her, the venerable Bishops of the entire Catholic world have humbly prayed the Sovereign Pontiff, in their name and in that of all
the faithful confided to their care, to deign to
declare St. Joseph Patron of the Catholic
Church. These prayers having been renewed
with still greater urgency at the time of the
Œcumenical Vatican Council, our Holy Father Pius IX., profoundly moved at the late
deplorable events, and wishing to place himself
and all the faithful in a special manner under
the all-powerful patronage of the holy Patri-

arch St. Joseph, has deigned to grant the wishes of the venerable Bishops. For this reason he has solemnly declared St. Joseph Patron of the Catholic Church; he has decreed that the feast of this Saint, on the 19th of March, should be henceforth raised to the position of a double of the first class, though without an octave, on account of Lent. He has also prescribed that the declaration thus made by the present decree of the Sacred Congregation of Rites should be published on the day consecrated to the Immaculate Conception of the Virgin Mother of God, the Spouse of the most chaste Joseph; and to this no one must raise any obstacle.

The 8th December of the year 1870.

(Signed) CONSTANTINE, Bishop of Ostia and Velletri.

CARD. PATRIZI, Prefect of the Sacred Congregation of Rites.

D. BARTOLINI, Secretary.

INTRODUCTION.

GOD seems to have reserved the devotion to St. Joseph for the terrible days of struggle and trial through which we are now passing.

To us who have the happiness to believe, it is evident that the misfortunes which we deplore to-day are the punishment of our sins; and if we wish to seek the reasons for our moral degradation, we shall find that they may be summed up under the following heads:

1st, Our forgetfulness of God; and 2dly, our neglect of domestic virtues.

The true spirit of Christianity only exists now in exceptional souls; and the peace and happiness of families are destroyed by self-ishness and egotism.

Now, the Saints, in the order of Provi-dence, are not only our protectors and inter-

cessors before God, but they should also be
our models; and the best way of honouring
them is by reproducing their noble qualities
in ourselves.

St. Joseph, to whom this Month is dedi-
cated by the Church, is the patron of the
hidden life. During the thirty years that
he shared with Mary the society of Jesus at
Nazareth, he lived continually in the presence
of God; while the spirit of faith directed all
his actions.

On the other hand, he is looked upon as
the model of a head of a family, and Nazareth as the school where we may learn, better
than anywhere else, those hidden and humble
virtues which form the great charm of family
life, and give such eloquence and force to the
teachings of both father and mother.

Let this, then, be the object of our pious
Meditations during these thirty-one days:
to seek, in the life of the glorious Patriarch
St. Joseph, an efficacious remedy for our
dissipation of mind and heart; and the way
to come back to that holy and happy family
life, which is the sole means of regenerating

society. Then, full of confidence in him, who only a few months ago was declared the Protector of the Universal Church by the highest moral and religious authority which exists here below, we will ask him perseveringly to help us by his powerful intercession, so that our Meditations may bring forth fruit in our actions; and that each day may see us advancing, step by step, in that perfect path in which he has preceded us.

All the perfections of St. Joseph are summed up in one word: ' *he was a just man.*'

This word 'just' may be taken in two different senses. A just man is one who possesses all Christian virtues. To be just, is to render to every one his due. And it is on this acceptation of the term that we shall principally dwell.

Our misfortune is to reverse the order of God's Providence. We attach great importance to trifling things, neglecting those which are essential. We forget that one thing only is necessary : to work out our own salvation and that of others.

We shall be just towards God and give

Him His due, by the practice of humility, faith, hope, and charity ; by prayer, and by obedience.   We shall be just towards our neighbour by fulfilling the duties of our station, both towards our families and towards society.

May St. Joseph, in whose honour we undertake this work, bless our efforts by making them useful to the souls of others.

MADAME DE GENTELLES.

AN

Abridgment of the Life of St. Joseph,

TAKEN FROM THE GOSPELS, AND THE FATHERS OF
THE CHURCH.

IT has appeared to us useful, while publishing these little Meditations for each day of the month of March, to precede them by a short Life of St. Joseph.

As we shall often have occasion to remark in meditating on the virtues of our glorious Patriarch, it has pleased our Lord to shroud his earthly career in mystery and silence. We know very little indeed of the events in his life. The Gospel has only given us one or two of those leading characteristics which make him so worthy of imitation. We have gathered from passages in the writings of the Fathers and of the Sacred Orators who have been pleased to glorify St. Joseph by their works, such details as may elucidate his his-

tory as far as we can; only regretting that
the scope of this little book precludes our
doing more than just plucking a flower, here
and there, from this fruitful garden.

When the time predestined by God for
the miraculous Incarnation of His Son was
come, His providential designs were realised
in the persons of Mary and of Joseph, whom
the Creator had chosen to be, in the eyes of
men, the spouse of the Virgin Mother and
the father of our Lord. He was, like Mary,
of the royal blood of David; his piety and
virtues had paved the way for the sublime
mission which was reserved to him.

Mary accepted him as her spouse, and
went to live in the humble house of Nazareth.

The Gospel tells us of the manner in which
the Angel reassured St. Joseph at the moment when, surprised at a mystery which he
could not understand, he was disposed to
leave the Virgin: 'Joseph, son of David,
fear not to take unto thee Mary thy wife,
for that which is conceived in her is of the
Holy Ghost' (St. Matt. i. 20).

St. Chrysostom remarks that, in the Gospels, St. Joseph appears always in the character of Father: 'It is to him alone that the Angel revealed the perils of the Holy Child, and it is to him that the time of the return from Egypt is announced. Jesus reverences and obeys him; and it is he who directs all His actions, as having the principal charge of the Child.' But to return to the Gospel narrative: 'And it came to pass that in those days there went out a decree from Cesar Augustus that the whole world should be enrolled. This enrolling was first made by Cyrinus, the Governor of Syria. And all went to be enrolled, every one into his own city. And Joseph also went up from Galilee, out of the city of Nazareth, into Judea, to the city of David, which is called Bethlehem, because he was of the house and family of David, to be enrolled with Mary his espoused wife, who was with child. And it came to pass that when they were there, her days were accomplished that she should be delivered. And she brought forth her first-born Son, and wrapped Him up in swaddling clothes, and laid Him in a manger, because there was no room for them in the inn' (St. Luke ii. 1-7).

The Angels appeared to the shepherds who were guarding their flocks near Bethlehem. They announced to them the birth of the Divine Child, and when these heavenly messengers had left them, the shepherds said one to another: ' Let us go over to Bethlehem, and let us see this word that is come to pass, which the Lord hath showed to us. And they came with haste; and they found Mary and Joseph, and the Infant lying in the manger' (St. Luke ii. 17).

God having thus chosen St. Joseph to be the coöperator in the work of the Redemption, as St. Bernard writes, He willed that he should be present at the birth of his son, and should hear himself the testimony of the shepherds when they came to adore the Saviour.

' And after eight days were accomplished that the child should be circumcised, his name was called Jesus, which was so called by the Angel before He was conceived in the womb' (St. Luke ii. 21).

' And after the days of her purification according to the law of Moses were accomplished, they carried Him to Jerusalem to present Him to the Lord. As it is written in the law, ... and to offer a sacrifice, . . . a pair of turtle-doves or two young pigeons. And behold, there was a man in Jerusalem named Simeon, and this man was just and devout, waiting for the consolation of Israel; and the Holy Ghost was in him. And he had received an answer from the Holy Ghost that he should not see death before he had seen the Christ of the Lord. And he came by the Spirit into the Temple. And when His parents brought in the Child Jesus, to do for Him according to the custom of the law, he also took Him into his arms, and blessed God and said: Now Thou dost dismiss Thy servant, O Lord, according to Thy word, in peace; because my eyes have seen Thy salvation, which Thou hast prepared before the face of all people : a light to the revelation of the gentiles, and the glory of Thy people Israel. And His father and mother were wondering at those things which were spoken concerning Him, and Simeon blessed them' (St. Luke ii. 22-34). Guided by a miraculous star, the Magi came from the east to adore the Divine Child, and when they had returned to their own country another way, to avoid the wiles of the king, God, knowing the designs of Herod, who feared to lose his kingdom, sent an Angel to Joseph, who said to him : ' Arise, and take the Child and His Mother, and fly into Egypt, and be there until I shall tell thee. For it will come to pass that Herod will seek the Child to destroy Him' (St. Matt. ii. 13). And Joseph, rising at once, took the Child and His Mother, by night, and fled into Egypt.

' Without losing a moment,' says St. Alphonse de Liguori, ' he hastily gathered together as many of his tools as he could carry, foreseeing that they would be useful to him in Egypt for the maintenance of his little family. Mary, on her side, took her Child in her arms, with such little things as He required, and so the two started in the middle of the night, like poor pilgrims,

to undertake this long and perilous journey,
having to traverse the vast desert which
separates Syria from Egypt, and knowing
that they should find among that barbarous
and unknown people neither relations nor
friends.'

'On their arrival, they took refuge in a
little town of the Thebaïd, named Helio-
polis, and there, hiring a small house, they
lived for seven years, as poor exiles from
their native land, deprived of every comfort. How did they exist during this time?
Did they beg? According to the tradition, our Lady worked and spun to supply
their daily needs and those of her Son.
What a sight! The queen of this world
compelled to toil at her needle to feed the
Creator of the universe, from His love of
holy poverty! How many privations and
mortifications these poor exiles must have
had to bear! For the Divine Master did
not come into the world to escape such
trials, but rather to meet them. And if,
sometimes, the Child-God, suffering the
pangs of hunger, asked for bread, and that

His Mother had none to give Him, what agony both to her heart and to that of St. Joseph! Mary strove to console her Son by tender words, while she redoubled her toil to gain enough for His support, and even took from her own slender meals what was necessary to feed Jesus. . . . Joseph, who was a carpenter, worked likewise at his trade, and so helped to supply their wants.' (Ludolphe de Saxe.)

But the hour was come for them to leave Egypt and return to their own country; and so God again sent His Angel to Joseph, saying:

'Arise, and take the Child and His Mother, and go into the land of Israel; for they are dead that sought the life of the Child.' 'Who arose and took the Child and His Mother, and came into the land of Israel. But hearing that Archelaus reigned in Judea in the room of Herod his father, he was afraid to go thither; and being warned in sleep, retired into the quarters of Galilee. And coming, he dwelt in a city called Nazareth, that it might be fulfilled which was said by the prophets: 'That He shall be called a Nazarite' (St. Matt. ii. 20-23). 'And the Child grew, and waxed strong, full of wisdom, and the grace of God was in Him' (St. Luke ii. 40). Look attentively upon this little family, blessed above all others, yet practising such rigid poverty, and leading so humble a life. Mary preparing the meals of her husband and Son, and doing all the other work of the house, for they had no servant. Pity this divine Virgin there, toiling with her own hands; and pity her Son, Jesus Christ our Lord, who helped her to the utmost of His childish power, and strove to spare her all the work He could, for as He said Himself: 'The Son of Man is not come to be ministered unto, but to minister' (St. Matt. xx. 28).

In consequence, may it not be presumed that He helped His Mother in laying their frugal table, and in all other domestic occupations? Contemplate Him fulfilling in His home the most menial offices, and think of His Virgin Mother, who shared them with

Him.   Fancy them all three every day
sitting down together to their humble meal,
which did not consist of any choice or delicate dishes, but of the plainest and coarsest
food.   Listen to their conversation; their
words, far from being idle and frivolous, are
full of wisdom and of the Spirit of God.
Their souls are thus fed like their bodies.
Watch them, after a short time of recreation, retiring each one to his little room to
take the necessary rest.   Consider Jesus,
the Divine Master of the world, who every
night, after prolonging His prayers to a late
hour, was content with a bed as humble and
wretched as could be found among the poor-
est of the people.' (St. Bonaventura.)

'And when He was twelve years old,
they going up into Jerusalem, according to
the custom of the feast, and having fulfilled
the days, when they returned, the Child
Jesus remained in Jerusalem, and His parents knew it not.   And thinking that He
was in the company, they came a day's journey, and sought Him among their kinsfolk
and acquaintance; and not finding Him,

they returned to Jerusalem, seeking Him.
And it came to pass that after three days
they found Him in the Temple, sitting in
the midst of the doctors, hearing them and
asking them questions. And all that heard
Him were astonished at His wisdom and
answers. And seeing Him they wondered.
And His Mother said to Him: Son, why
hast Thou done so to us? Behold, Thy father and I have sought Thee sorrowing.
And He said to them: How is that you
sought Me? Did you not know that I
must be about My Father's business? And
they understood not the word that He spoke
unto them. And He went down with them
and came to Nazareth, and was subject to
them' (St. Luke ii. 44-51).

'Is it necessary to tell that Jesus was, towards Joseph, the best and the most tender
of Sons, showing him a respect, a submission, and a perfect obedience in all things,
as to a much-loved father? O, roof! O,
walls! O, happy enclosure! which sheltered
this august family, and which were witnesses of their labours, of their recreations,

of the holy conversations between Jesus, Mary, and Joseph, tell us how often Joseph, to refresh himself after his fatigues, repeated the sweet name of Jesus, and with what respectful eagerness Jesus ran to answer his call, saying to him with a celestial joy in His countenance: "Here I am, My father, what do you want? What do you command?" Joseph, whose humility was so deep, that the four Evangelists do not report one single word uttered by him—Joseph, it seems to me, to grant the desire of Jesus, must often have said to Him, "Come, my Son, help me in this work." And Jesus helped him, doing everything with such grace and modesty, that all the inhabitants of Nazareth ran to Joseph's shop to see this wonderful Child at work. But they were not alone; all the prophets ran also from a great distance to see Him.'* O, happy Joseph, exclaims the Prophet Isaiah, this Child who works for thee, and calls thee father, is 'Wonderful, Counsellor, God the mighty, the Father of the world to come, the Prince

* St. Bonaventura.

of Peace, the Angel of the Great Council'
(Isaiah ix. 6).

He whom you look upon as your Son,
writes the Prophet Micheas, 'is to be the
Ruler in Israel; and His going forth is
from the beginning, from the days of eternity' (Micheas v. 2). And again the royal
prophet speaks of Him as of one ' to whom
the whole earth belongs, and all that it contains.'

Although we do not know exactly the
date of St. Joseph's death, all tradition
agrees in placing it during the last year of
our Saviour's private life. Had he been
still on earth at the time of the passion of
Jesus, we should have seen him at the foot
of the Cross, and our Lord would not have
needed to confide His Mother to the care
of St. John.

'Let us consider this blessed Patriarch,
in the arms of Jesus and Mary, at the moment of giving up his soul to his Creator.
See him stretched on his poor bed, Jesus
on one side and Mary on the other, surrounded by a multitude of angels, archangels, and

seraphim, who, with a respectful attention, are waiting to receive this holy soul. O, God, who shall tell us with what feelings, at this supreme moment, Joseph took a last leave of Jesus and Mary ? What acts of thankfulness, of supplication, of humility, on the part of this holy old man ! His eyes and his heart speak, only his tongue is silent. But how much there is in his silence! He looks at Mary, and Mary at him; and with what love and veneration ! Then he turns his dying eyes on Jesus, and Jesus returns the look, but with what tenderness ! He takes the hand of Jesus, and presses it to his heart, and covers it with kisses, and bedews it with his tears, and says to Him, from time to time, less with his lips than in his heart: "My Son, my much-loved Son, I recommend my soul to Thee !" And then, placing that hand on his heart, he falls into a swoon of love. Ah, Joseph ! if you could but keep fast hold of that hand, which is life, you would not die ! O, how sweet it would be to die, holding the hand of Jesus !

'The soul is on the point of leaving the body; it has already half taken flight; but at the sight of Jesus and Mary it pauses: it cannot break its chain. I repeat, Joseph, if you do not cease to look upon Him who is your life, you cannot die. Tender and divine Redeemer Jesus, holy Mary, Joseph cannot quit this land of exile if you will not give him leave! Jesus lifts His hand. He blesses and embraces His much-loved father, and Joseph expires in the arms of Jesus' (Blessed Leonard of Port Maurice).

'A Saint who had so loved in life could only die of love, for his soul could not love Jesus enough amidst the distractions of this life; and having fulfilled the duty required of him, in tending the childhood of his Lord, what remained but that he should say to the Eternal Father: "I have finished the work which Thou gavest me to do" (St. John xvii. 4). And to the Son: "My Child, as your heavenly Father intrusted your body into my hands on the day that you came into the world, so on this day of my departure from this world, I remit my spirit into Yours."

'Such, I imagine, was the death of this great Patriarch, the most noble death of all, due to the most noble life which any creature had ever led—a death which angels themselves would covet if they were capable of dying.' (St. François de Sales.)

FIRST DAY.

' Be little in your own eyes, so that you may be great in the eyes of God.' ST. AUGUSTINE.

THE work of our sanctification may be looked upon as a spiritual edifice, which we are all bound to raise in our souls. Well, the first thing when one wants to build, is to lay a good foundation. This is an essential condition of durability; and therefore we place first the Christian virtue of Humility, which is the foundation without which no real virtue can exist.

St. Gregory calls humility the germ and root of all good; and this again is a very true figure, for the root is buried in the earth and hidden from our eyes, although its action is visible enough. It draws up the nourishing sap from the soil, and gives that fresh foliage and those brilliant flowers

c

which would soon wither and die if the stem
were separated from the root.

But how shall we define humility ?   In
one word : humility is the truth applied to
the knowledge of ourselves. ' To know oneself,' says St. Augustine, ' is the highest
practice of wisdom.' ' My Lord, who art
Thou ? and what am I ?'   There are, alas !
many men, who, the prey to self-love, arrive
at the term of their career without ever
knowing themselves, even for a moment.
They have lived amidst the illusions of the
world, and of those fumes of vain-glory,
which will prepare for them such a terrible
awakening at the day of judgment.

To arrive at this knowledge of oneself,
we must, armed with the light of faith, resolutely descend into the depths of our
hearts, and examine the principle and motive
of each of our actions, remembering that, as
a Christian philosopher has remarked, God
does not see things from the same point of
view as men.   His approbation cannot be
measured by that of any creature.   Many
acts, which are praised and admired by those

who surround us, have perhaps no merit at
all in the eyes of our Lord; and we must
own that, in many circumstances, we should
blush indeed if it were given to our brother
to probe the depths of our hearts deeply
enough to discover the hidden motive of
such and such an action, which he appre-
ciates because he only sees the exterior.

Self-knowledge is to form a just estimate
of the different qualities we find in ourselves;
for humility is not the negation of the good
which we may discover; it consists, according to St. Thomas, in distinguishing what is
of God, and what is the result of the free
exercise of our will. In fact, the exterior
advantages of beauty, grace, strength, &c.,
are the personal *gifts* which God has bestowed on each one of us. It is the same
with intellectual qualities. God has meted
out to each a certain amount of intelligence,
cleverness, memory, &c. To attribute these
gifts to ourselves is to be out of the realm of
truth. It is the same, and with still greater
reason, with the spiritual graces which God
has granted to us. By thus carrying on our

self-examination with all the sincerity of a straightforward, honest heart, we shall inevitably arrive at the conclusion of the prophet, that of ourselves we are but dust and ashes, inclined to evil from our earliest infancy, and capable of committing the greatest faults. But this appreciation is not enough; it is only the first and most easy step or degree of humility; 'for a man may have the greatest mistrust of himself, believe and feel himself below others, and yet pride may be the ruling passion of his life. If his weaknesses only disturb him; if he makes no efforts to struggle against them; if he indulges in hatred against those who surpass him; if he only seeks obscurity lest he should be exposed to humiliating comparisons, he is not humble of heart, but full of pride.'

Humility is not an instinct, but the result of serious reflection; and the second degree consists in accepting willingly and without interior revolt the unfavourable judgments which our neighbour may pass upon us, and even his contempt.

Humanity fell from a pride which wished to raise itself above the condition in which God had placed man, after having created him out of nothing; and our only chance of salvation is in taking a directly opposite course to that which made the misery of our first parents. There is no doubt that it costs something to our nature to be abased, to consent to be forgotten, judged of unfavourably, and despised; but therein lies the merit. As St. Augustine remarks, Jesus said to His Disciples, ' You wish to be exalted; well, I promise it to you.' He joined example to precept. He descended from Heaven and took upon Him the form of a servant. He loved and sought for humiliation. He was born in a stable. The first thirty years of His life were spent under the humble roof of a workman. During His public life He was exposed to the contradictions of men; dragged like a culprit through the streets of Jerusalem; treated as a madman or a fool; condemned to death for imaginary crimes; and, finally, He expired on a cross between two thieves. He

has, then, the right to ask us to follow in
His steps. The way is open, let us walk in
it with courage; let us leave the judgments
of men, who are nothing in the sight of God,
and let us gather up the words of Mary,
that most humble of created beings, when
she bursts forth in that hymn of thanksgiving which is already a cry of triumph : ' My
soul doth magnify the Lord, and my spirit
hath rejoiced in God my Saviour. For He
hath regarded the humility of His hand-
maid: for behold, from henceforth all generations shall call me blessed. For He that
is mighty hath done great things unto me;
and holy is His name. And His mercy is
from generation to generation unto them
that fear Him. He hath showed strength
with His arm; He hath scattered the proud
in the imagination of their heart. He hath
put down the mighty from their seat, and
hath exalted the humble.'

Let us humble ourselves, then, by the
practice of humility to conquer back the
Throne in Heaven, which should have been
our eternal portion had not pride deprived

us of it. Let us with joy take the lowest place, so that the Divine Master, on coming to the wedding feast, may say, ' Friend, go up higher.'

The practice of humility is hard in the beginning; but the more progress we make, the easier and sweeter it will become. It is thus that the Saints came not only to accept humiliations, but to rejoice in them. The servant is not greater than his master; and is there not a real satisfaction in seeing oneself treated like Him, whose banner it is an honour to follow ?

God sometimes gives to the souls of His servants an ardent thirst for humiliations and the contempt of the world. To attain to this degree of virtue should be the object of our efforts, and would bring us great peace and ineffable joy.

SECOND DAY.

HUMILITY (*continued*).

'Through humility, man inclines himself respect-
fully before God, and before men in the sight of
God.' ST. THOMAS.

IT is not enough to recognise that we must
be humble on principle; that is, that we
must keep our place, accept contempt on the
part of our equals, and even aim at liking
this contempt itself. We must resolutely
enter into the practice of this admirable virtue, and ask ourselves in what way a woman
of the world may climb up the different degrees or steps of humility, and thus acquire
a liberty of spirit, and a joy and interior
peace, which are already a precious reward
for our efforts.

There are two great obstacles to our progress in humility—pride and vanity.

We may define pride as an exaggerated

esteem of ourselves; and the great remedy
for this fatal inclination is prayer, joined to
an attentive consideration of our own de-
fects and short-comings.

Let us, then, ask of God each day the
grace to know ourselves, and courageously
to scrutinise our motives and intentions.

Vanity is the desire to be highly esteemed.
It is easier to root out pride than vanity.

This each of us knows by her own experience. When we have humbled ourselves
before God and, assisted at the Holy Sacrifice, when we have thoroughly recognised
our nothingness in His sight and our im-
potence for good, and we then return to our
homes and family, occasions, perhaps, will
at once arise for attracting observation, or
provoking some praise or admiration; and
it will require a real interior struggle to be
able to triumph over this temptation. We
shall feel in the same way if we find our
motives misconstrued, our actions misinter-
preted, or harsh judgments passed upon us.
Ah, it is then that we realise how strongly
we still cling to human approbation; how

anxious we are to fill an honourable place in
the world, and one which we fancy we deserve. And God only knows to what length
a great number of women push these pre-
tensions, even among those who make a
great profession of leading a Christian life.

For such women a large field is required.
It is not enough for them to be admired:
they wish to have the exclusive privilege of
being so; they desire to surpass all others
in beauty and luxury; and when all hope
of such successes is over, they aspire to
wield the sceptre of intellect, or wit. Vanity
perverts the heart. Do not venture to talk
before a woman who is full of herself and
of her own merits, of the charms and good .
qualities of another woman; your praises
will be quite enough to give her a horror
of her. She cannot bear a rival; she alone
must bear away the palm. Ah, how contrary such feelings are to genuine humility!

Let us conclude by meditating on the admirable example given us by St. Joseph in
this respect, that man so humble above all
others.

' There is no doubt,' says St. Francis de Sales, 'that St. Joseph was greater than David, and wiser than Solomon. But as the palm-tree does not put forth her flowers until the moment when the burning sun makes them blossom, in the same way the soul of this just man hides the flower of his virtues under the veil of holy humility, until the death of our Lord makes them shine forth in all their splendour. O, my brethren, I do not doubt that the angels, in an ecstasy of admiration, came by troops to see and admire the poverty and abjection under which St. Joseph concealed the greatest virtues and the highest dignities.'

The son of a king, called by God to fill the most sublime mission upon earth, after that of Mary, Joseph spent his whole life under the mantle of humility.

We are ignorant of the day of his birth; that of his death is also unknown; and we are obliged to content ourselves with pious suppositions as to the details of an existence, the least particulars of which would have been full of interest to us.

He passed unperceived among his contemporaries; that poor little house of Nazareth, the subject of constant admiration to the whole celestial court, is, as it were, altogether hidden from the eyes of men.

- Joseph seeks not for their esteem or their praise. Neither would add to that greatness and nobility which are the result of his eminent virtues. Would they have added anything either to the unmixed happiness with which he accomplished his task? When, at Bethlehem, he found every door closed against him, do you think for a moment that he allowed his mind to dwell on the humiliation of being thus treated? O, no; in his troubles, as in his joys, he had but one object, and that was God.

We also, like St. Joseph, have our Nazareth; and like him, also, a holy mission to fulfil.

Has not all experience shown us, that there is no real happiness save in the bosom of our families? To be simple, humble, loving, devoted, and modest in our homes, may be difficult or even impossible to a worldly

woman; but not to a Christian who endea-
vours to practise the maxims of Faith,
Hope, and Charity, and to follow the example of our holy Patriarch.

THIRD DAY.

'To have faith is to believe what we cannot see; and
the reward of faith will be to see what we have
believed.' St. Augustine.

FAITH is a virtue and a gift of God, by
which we believe in Him, and in all that
He has revealed to His Church.

The first act of faith was shown by Adam
and Eve when they had confessed their fault
to God; and followed their humiliation before Him.

The mercy of the Creator had triumphed
over His justice. He drove from His presence, and excluded from the Garden of
Eden, the guilty pair who had disobeyed
His commandment; but He vouchsafed to
them the promise of a Redeemer, who should
be their beacon to guide their steps in the
land of their exile.

In Paradise, in the days of their inno-
cence, they saw God. One of the most
terrible consequences of sin was the darken-
ing of their minds. It is night in their
souls: they will no longer see God; but
they will believe without seeing until the
day when, purified by a long and painful
trial, they will at last see Him in whom
they have believed.

And this intellectual darkness is so evi-
dently the consequence of our moral corrup-
tion, that the more a man gives himself up
to his passions, the more his religious belief
is impaired. The history of the ancients
who fell into idolatry, and of these last
days wholly given up to materialism, are
the melancholy proofs of this.

The more, on the contrary, the soul is
purified by virtue and suffering, the easier
faith becomes. We shall only see God
when the earthly links which bind us here
below shall be broken; for human nature
is not capable of sustaining such a ray of
glory, which makes St. Thomas exclaim,

that 'the Divinity is obscure by reason of too much light.'

We read in Exodus that Moses said one day to God, 'Lord, show me Thy glory;' and that He replied: 'I will show thee all good, ... but thou canst not see My face, for man shall not see Me and live. . . . . But when My glory shall pass, I will set thee in a hole of the rock and protect thee with My right hand till I pass, and thou shalt see as a last ray of My glory' (Exodus xxxiii. 20-22). And we know that this last ray of light so illumined the face of Moses, that he was obliged to cover his head with a veil when he spoke to the Jews.

There are solemn moments in the Christian life when God passes so near us, that it seems as if the cloud which envelops Him had become transparent. 'Faith then becomes the sensible presence of God in our hearts' (Pascal).

'This great virtue,' writes l'Abbé Perreyre, 'does not confine itself to barren evidence. It goes beyond. It seizes truth:

as yet unperceived. It enters without fear
into the region of things invisible, and fixing its desires on future promises, it seems
to possess already the fruition of its hopes.'

This is the excellence of supernatural
faith, which St. Paul has defined in that
grand text: 'Faith is the substance of
things to be hoped for, the evidence of
things that appear not' (Hebrews xi. 1).
The hour of a sudden return to God, a conversion, in fact, is often the occasion of
one of those lightning flashes which illu-
mine the night of life. Saul, struck down
on his way to Damascus; Augustine in the
garden of Cassiaco, when the mysterious
' Tolle lege' sounded in his ears; Father
Ratisbon in the church of S. Andrea delle
Fratte, are all striking examples of this.

Let us listen to the words of a famous
woman to whom our Lord thus spoke, after
she had given herself up to all the pleasures
of a deceitful world:

'It seemed as if a curtain were drawn,
which hung before the eyes of my soul.
The charms of truth were revealed to me in

a new light. Faith, which had been dead
and buried under my passions, woke again;
and I felt myself like one who, after a long
dream, in which she had fancied herself
great, happy, and highly thought of by
everybody, wakes all of a sudden and finds
herself loaded with chains, covered with
wounds, worn out with fatigue, and shut
up in a dark prison' (Madame de Longue-
ville).

Again, in presence of a great sorrow,
when our heart is torn by a cruel separation, and our tears flow beside the bier which
contains all that we love best on earth, God
draws near, and through faith fills our souls
with supreme consolation. We are tempted
then to exclaim with a venerable Bishop:
' Never did I feel so vividly as in presence
of that tomb, the belief in that which is beyond. Never did the veil between the two
worlds appear to me more transparent; never
did I have such an intuition of our immortality' (Mgr. Gerbet).

At Bethlehem, in Egypt, at Nazareth,
the divinity of the Word was hidden from

the eyes of Mary and Joseph, in the person
of Jesus under the form of a little child;
but may we not suppose that the veil which
hid His divinity became often so transparent
to them, that their act of faith was transformed into an act of love?

All men live two lives, the natural and
the supernatural. The first may be defined
to be the things we see and feel, and which
daily pass before our eyes. The supernatural
life, on the contrary, is hidden from the eyes
of men, and its operations are invisible to
our bodily senses.

Time is only a prelude to eternity. Well,
this veil or cloud, of which we spoke before,
floats between our soul and this supernatural
world, which is our true home. Here, again,
we find ourselves in presence of faith: we
must believe without seeing; believe not
only in God, in His existence, in His perfections, but in His Word, which is the formal expression of His divine will as regards
us.

When our Divine Master traversed the
provinces of Judea, and by His power the

dead were restored to life, the blind received
their sight, the deaf heard, and the dumb
spoke, cries of admiration burst forth on
every side. The Jews acknowledged His
power, and wished to make Him a king;
but yet, far from ranging themselves under
His banner, they became His enemies, because they feared the severity of His doctrine.

Women in our days do not lift themselves up against God; they even accept
such religious practices as cost them little.
But how many amongst them set aside everything which goes against their tastes and
inclinations, or which involves a sacrifice?
We are keenly sensible of this tendency in
those near and dear to us, for whom we so
earnestly plead for light and courage to overcome the obstacles which stand in the way
of their conversion. With them is it not
the heart that doubts? Let us pray—that
is our great resource. Let us implore of
God to grant them the light of faith, and
to destroy all those stumbling-blocks which
thwart the operations of grace in their souls.
And then let us take courage, remembering

the example of St. Monica, and the consoling words of the holy Bishop : ' It cannot
be that the son of so many tears should
perish.'

FOURTH DAY.

FAITH (*continued*).

'The just shall live by faith.' ST. PAUL.

To live by faith is to make it the motive power of our souls, and to regulate all our actions by this standard.

Faith gives us, in three short sentences, the true secret of life:

1. A duty to fulfil.
2. A cross to carry.
3. An apostolate to exercise.

We must start from this point if we wish to ask ourselves, as before God: Are we really living by faith?

Life is duty; that is, it is a succession of actions dictated to us by certain positive laws contained in that Christian code which we call the Gospel.

These duties are serious: we cannot be wanting in them without being gravely culpable; and on our observance of them depends our eternal happiness or misery. Since the sin of our first parents, life is less an enjoyment than an expiation. That seems hard to us; our feelings revolt against the idea, but we cannot help ourselves. It is a religious truth which we cannot deny: life is an expiation, a trial, and a cross; in a word, it is an apostolate.

The soul that believes, wishes to impart this precious gift of faith to those that have not yet been thus enlightened. Nothing costs her to arrive at this end: she thirsts for the salvation of her brethren. Willingly, like the Apostle, would she become for them ' anathema maranatha.'

Without doubt, human frailty is great. We may stumble and fall in our course; slacken our speed in ascending the ladder of perfection. But the important thing is to set a high standard before us, and regularly to strive to act up to it, guided by the light of faith, which alone can preserve us amidst the rocks and shoals of our mortal course. If we do not understand that this is the object of life—to glorify our good God and work for Him—we are outside the divine plan, and do not deserve existence.

We are in the midst of a world of which the usages and maxims are completely opposed to the spirit of Jesus Christ. The current against us is strong, and the misfortune of many women is to let themselves be carried away by it, according to the common expression—not to have courage and strength enough to say: '*I will go so far, and no further.*'

To live *in* the world and yet not be *of* it: such is the advice of the Apostle.

It is faith, writes St. Augustine, which elevates our life and makes it straightforward and good. Without it we can but drag on our weary way, leaving rags of our clothing on every thorn by the wayside; not knowing from whence we came or whither we are going. How empty and poor is the life of a fashionable worldly woman, who has never felt the vivifying influence of faith! To soar upwards is a necessity of the soul, and thus alone can we live in a higher region, leaving

on one side the miserable cares and troubles
of this wretched life, which otherwise would
hopelessly weigh us down. The dove, when
it left the ark, could not stop on the earth;
and so we, by union with God and the
realisation of His presence, may feel the
nothingness of worldly pleasures, and taste,
in anticipation, the happiness and joys of
heaven. It is said in Holy Scripture that
crooked ways are an abomination to the
Lord, but that the path of the upright is
His delight. Let us, then, go with loving
confidence to Him, without allowing ourselves to be diverted from our course by the
things of this world. Life is a race, where
all must run and fight; only let us be sure
that we do not run in vain. Let us not
either be laggards on the road. The day is
far spent, the night is at hand; very soon
that day will dawn which knows of no decline.

Unless faith be the groundwork of our
lives, no virtue can be solid or real. It is
only faith which gives us courage to uproot
that deplorable egotism which spoils all our

good and holy intentions. Was it not by striving constantly to please God that the early Christians won their crowns? Their heroic courage, their constancy in the midst of the most fearful tortures—what were these but the admirable fruits of that faith which we share in common with them? Only the other day, have we not seen generous souls, priests of the Lord, offer their lives as proofs of their invincible faith? But for such sacrifices, the most noble which man can offer to God, a preparation is required, and that preparation must be found in the faithful performance of duty.

Courage, then! Even should God not demand a bloody sacrifice at our hands, the hour is not far distant when we must leave this world. May we then be able to repeat, after St. Francis of Sales, the noble words which he pronounced on his deathbed:

'I have always believed with the simplicity of a child; it was my greatest happiness to believe. I die in that Catholic faith which I have loved, which I have preached, and for which I would gladly give my life!'

FIFTH DAY.

HOPE.

'We live by hope.' St. Paul.

Hope is our life; and this is so true that there are men who voluntarily sacrifice their own existence and put an end to their own lives because they are without hope.

Youth believes easily in a happy future; it is the age of illusions, but as the years pass by, these illusions disappear and vanish one by one, like the leaves of the forest carried away by the autumn wind.

The hour of thorough disenchantment is a terrible one, and if God does not vouchsafe a ray of heavenly hope to the soul to whom the world has nothing more to offer, the dark night of despair sets in.

What, then, is hope?

It is awaiting the realisation of that which we wish for.

The man of the world sets his hope on the things of this world; he desires honours, riches, pleasure; he thinks to attain happiness by the sole possession of these fragile and deceptive things; but he is following a vain phantom, he is leaning on a broken reed which will assuredly bruise his hand, and everywhere will he meet with deception; for our hearts are not created to find entire satisfaction here below. 'Mere human hope, trembling, timid, doubtful as it is, without support and without foundation, cannot set the heart at rest, because it holds it ever suspended over an uncertain future.'

'The soul requires an anchor, to use St. Paul's expression. Imagine a vessel far away from the port and the shore, tossing about upon an unknown sea. If a storm comes on, if the sun is covered over with clouds, then the pilot, uncertain as to his course, and fearing lest the violence of the waves and of the winds should drive it against the rocks, orders the anchor to be thrown out, and that anchor upholds and

supports it even in the midst of the waves'
(Bossuet).

This anchor, of which Bossuet speaks, is
the image of another anchor, which cannot
deceive us; for this great God, this great
King of the world, whose promises we revere, being eternal and unchangeable, in
whose hands are the times and seasons,
can alone measure their course. And as the
future is no less His than the present, it follows that what He promises is no less certain than what He actually gives. Heaven
and earth will pass away, but His words will
not pass away; and since He is true, whether He gives or whether He promises, the
Christian has no less assurance in hope than
in fruition.

Christian hope, then, is a virtue, the first
object of which is the happiness of a future
life; that is to say, God possessed, known,
and loved, throughout all the years of eternity. Its second object is the necessary
grace in order that we may attain to our
supreme end.

God, who is infinitely good, would never

have put into our hearts the insatiable thirst
for happiness with which we are devoured,
had He not intended to satisfy it.

We were created to be happy. Faith
gives us the assurance of it, and hope, which
is the desire of faith, is intended to comfort
and uphold our souls amidst all the vicissi-
tudes of life.

What could have shaken the boundless confidence that St. Joseph had in God? Let us
recall to mind the mysteries of our Saviour's
life with which St. Joseph is associated. He
never stops to consider the human side of
things. He sets out for Bethlehem when
quiet and rest were apparently most desir-
able for our Blessed Lady; he goes into
exile without knowing how in that distant
land he will be able to provide for the wants
of Jesus and Mary. On his return to Judea,
he goes back to his work still upheld by
hope; and when, in the arms of Jesus and
Mary, he delivers up his pure and holy soul
to God, he falls asleep bearing away with
him into the grave the hope of a speedy
deliverance.

Many Christian souls are prone to a dangerous error; they confuse and mix up, so to say, earthly hopes with heavenly hopes.

It would be a work very profitable to our souls, were we to separate completely in our own minds those things which concern this present life, and those which have reference to the future.

We must remember that nowhere has God promised us the goods of this world, glory, riches, or pleasures. Neither has He promised to exempt us from the sufferings and the troubles which belong to our human nature: sickness, privations of every kind, may come upon us, death may carry away all that is dear to us here below. Let us remember the history of Job, and the great trials through which it pleased Almighty God that His servant should pass. It was at the very moment when the holy patriarch of Arabia was struck down by sickness of body, by the loss of his worldly goods, by the death of his children, and even by a sort of estrangement on the part of his wife, that, raising himself above all human considera-

tions, he exclaimed: ' Should the Lord take
away my life, I should not cease to hope in
Him; yet will I expose my ways to Him,
and He Himself will be my Saviour. For,
behold, short years pass away, and I am
walking in a path by which I shall not return; my spirit shall be wasted, my days
shall be shortened, and only the grave re-
maineth for me. I know that my Redeemer
liveth, and in the last day I shall rise out of
the earth, and in my flesh I shall see my
God, whom I myself shall see, and my eyes
shall behold, and not another. This my hope
is laid up in my bosom.'

It is not the recovery of his lost fortunes,
nor yet the consolations which he might
expect from his friends and relations, for
which this holy man of Idumea is longing;
he desires only the day of eternity, that
day which soon will dawn for him, and therefore it is that his hope will not be confounded.

A little while ago a young girl of fifteen
was within a few hours of her death; no
one liked to tell her of her danger, but she,

full of faith, inquired whether the hour of her departure was not at hand. Her piety being well known, she was told that perhaps that very evening she might be on her way to heaven. At this news she could no longer contain her joy, and there burst from her lips the most fervent expressions of rejoicing and thanksgiving. For, long ago, God alone had been the anchor of her hopes.

The lives of the Saints give us numberless examples of this burning desire for heaven. ' I die because I cannot die,' exclaims St. Theresa.

It is God's grace alone which can thus supernaturalise our feelings. With hope in our hearts, the whole aspect of life is changed. Sufferings and trials still remain, but far from being an obstacle to happiness, they become its source. There are no longer any inconsolable sorrows, for the Christian cannot mourn like those who have no hope.

SIXTH DAY.

ΠOPE (*continued*).

'Lord, I shall not be confounded if I have hoped
in Thee.' Ps.

WE sin against hope through presumption
and despair. It is presumptuous to suppose
that a certain end can be reached without
taking the proper means to attain it.

We have around us frequent examples of
this deplorable tendency, which is too often
an unfortunate characteristic of the young.
Destitute of experience, they reject good advice ; they are profoundly ignorant, and yet
believe they know everything; they fear
neither difficulties nor obstacles, and love
to put themselves on an equality with the
greatest intellects and the bravest hearts.

Like a traveller who undertakes a long
and dangerous journey without provisions
and unarmed, the presumptuous think they

will find in themselves all the resources
they may require.

Can one, then, wonder at so many self-
delusions, at so many falls?

And now that we see in what, taken
from a human point of view, this self-con-
fidence, of which we have so often deplored
the effects, consists, it is easy thoroughly to
understand what is called presumption from
a spiritual point of view.

It is hope which makes us believe that
with the help of the all - powerful grace,
which our Lord has purchased for us with
the price of His precious Blood, we shall
attain eternal happiness; and here is a two-
fold danger to be avoided: relying too much
on ourselves, and not having thorough and
entire confidence in God.

God will not save us alone, the concur-
rence of our own will is necessary; and if
we allow ourselves to remain in a state of
spiritual inactivity (of which the physical
immovability of certain inhabitants of the
East is an image), we shall not attain the end
to which we aspire. On the other hand, our

own efforts alone, however unceasing, could only produce a human result. In order that they may gain heaven for us, they must themselves be supernaturalised by grace.

We are certain to land in the harbour of salvation after the dangerous voyage of life, on the condition that we never lose sight of the end of our journey, and that we have our spiritual provisions always with us.

None will be lost for want of the grace which is necessary to save them; but many, . alas, will perish because they have neglected the precautions which Christian prudence should have suggested.

To love danger is to expose oneself to perish in it. How often has our Lord given us to understand that certain pleasures, certain companions, certain books, were hurtful to our souls! But we neglected the salutary warning; we had not the courage to deprive ourselves of some great pleasure, of some delightful conversation, or of some book which had attracted our curiosity; and so we fell, and we were surprised at

our fall. And soon sadness took possession
of our souls, and with sadness discouragement, which is the high road to despair;
the greatest of all sins, because we thereby outrage the goodness of God, which is
that one amongst His attributes which He
most loves to manifest to us, and to which
He wishes us to render homage by a boundless confidence. Sadness and discouragement, we should observe, are invariably the
consequences of presumption.

Were we but thoroughly convinced of
our weakness and incapacity, we should not
wonder at our frequent falls; but having
believed ourselves to be something, we are
dismayed when we discover that we are but
dust and ashes.

Let us examine how a soul, which has
relied too much on its own strength, begins,
little by little, first to have doubts of the
mercy of God, and finally of its own salvation. She had fancied that it would be an
easy matter to advance boldly in the path
of piety; soon, however, there came a fall.
What happens? Will this poor soul rise

up again? continue its course? begin again? No; surprised by a result so different from what she had expected, she gives way to unlimited sadness, and her previous state of exaggerated confidence in herself gives place to one of utter hopelessness, (a state no less harmful to the spiritual life,) until by almost insensible transitions she believes herself incapable of any fresh effort; and then the image of an inexorable God rises up in her soul and fills her with terror.

She feels as if she had been redeemed in vain. Heaven seems lost to her for ever, and she then pronounces the terrible words, 'There is no hope.' The work of the devil is thus accomplished, and by this means he succeeds in securing the death of a soul, which he could not otherwise have separated from God.

In order to combat so great an evil as discouragement, it must be vigorously fought against from the very beginning. We must never give way to this spiritual sadness, which soon brings us into a state of languor, incapacitating us for all that is good.

Whatever may be the number and the enormity of our sins, let us never forget that the mercy of God is always infinitely greater. It is an article of faith that the very least of our Lord's sufferings would have sufficed to redeem a thousand worlds infinitely more sinful than ours. As long as the breath is in our bodies we can be saved, and in the course of our whole life there never is one instant in which God is inexorable. To doubt His forgiveness, is to doubt His power. He has but one desire, which never changes: the desire to save His creatures and to make them happy.

He detests sin, but He never ceases to love the sinner; and in the Holy Scriptures He tells us that He desireth not the death of a sinner, but his conversion. Our Lord came to save those who were lost, and in the Gospels, our Divine Master shows Himself under the figures which are the most consoling to a guilty soul. He calls Himself the Father of the prodigal son, the Shepherd who bears on his shoulders the sheep that was lost; He breaketh not the bruised reed, nor quencheth the smoking flax.

He who created us knows our fragility and our weakness. Let us not, then, lose heart, however great may be our sinfulness! We wish to be saved; God desires it even more than we do ourselves; and what power could hinder the effect of His infinite mercy and our repentance at the hour of death?

The Christian, then, who goes along his road leaning on hope, possesses within himself an unquenchable spring of joy, which nothing can destroy. He is serving a Master of infinite goodness and of infinite power, and he is himself called to indescribable happiness. Let him, then, banish from his soul all those noxious vapours, which hide the end from his view. Whatever may be our trials and infirmities, serenity ought to be the constant state of our souls.

In our hours of sadness and discouragement, let us penetrate in spirit into that Cave of Bethlehem where He lay whose judgments we dread. Let us draw near to the manger, to Mary and to Joseph, and

with them let us adore this holy Child, who
is raising His hand to bless us. Why does
He lie there, the Eternal Word, the Son of
God—God Himself? Why does He offer Himself for our worship under the attractive form
of a little child? Is it not because He desires
that love shall prevail over fear, so that it
may be said of us, as it was of a celebrated
sinner : ' Much shall be forgiven her, because she hath loved much' ?

SEVENTH DAY.

ON THE LOVE OF GOD.

'Love begets love.' PROVERBS.

IN every human heart there exists a great capacity of love, and do what we will, our whole life is spent in trying to satisfy it; indeed, half the misfortunes which befall mankind proceed from the erroneous direction too often given to this faculty, to which God has given such a wonderful power.

In vain do we seek our happiness in the love of creatures. They can offer us nothing but disappointment, emptiness, and that hopeless *ennui* which is at the bottom of every human existence. The human heart is too large to be satisfied by passing and earthly affections. It was created to love God, and God alone can fill it. A well-known orator thus expresses the same thought, with all the eloquence which ever

characterises him : ' Love is so much a part
of our being, it is so nearly related to us,
that nothing is easier for us, or more natural to us, than to love !'

You rise as usual; the morning air is re-
dolent with the sweet perfumes of spring,
the trees are gently swayed by the soft wind;
you open your window, and a dreamy feeling
of happiness steals over you, and you long
to go forth and greet the new-born day,
steeping your every sense in light, and air,
and warmth. But God—God! is He less
to you than the wind, less than the air, less
than the light, less than the flower, that you
do not think of Him ?

' What is God ?'

God is our Creator, our Saviour, our Father; by His Incarnation He has made
Himself our brother, and He will be our reward for all eternity.

If it be true to say that love begets love,
how are we to respond to that love which
God has shown to us? We owe him everything : the air that we breathe, the life
which flows in our veins, our hopes of eter-

that He should die for those He loved; in leaving them He yet wished to remain amidst them. ' My delight,' He says, ' is to be with the children of men.' And the Holy Eucharist became the lasting memorial of the love of a God for His poor and weak creatures.

Jesus, therefore, has become our brother, the companion of our exile; and not only was He this in the far-off days, when He came down upon the earth to redeem our guilty race, but, O mystery of love! for the last two thousand years He has ever dwelt among us. The churches which contain our Incarnate God, though concealed under the fragile semblance of a little bread, are not far from our own homes, and yet the Divine Master still remains the *unknown* God! We are surprised when we hear God command us to love Him; and yet even the command is not obeyed. In truth, we present a mystery of ingratitude in return for so many mysteries of love.

Where are those fervent souls, those hearts of fire, who exclaimed, in the rapture of their love, ' God alone ! God alone !'—those who lived and died for Him ? St. Joseph was the first among men who loved the Incarnate Son of God; he loved Him as his son, as the Treasure of the world, confided to him by the Eternal Father, as his Creator, as his Redeemer, and as his God. Who can tell of the fervour of his devotion ? Mary and Joseph at the foot of the crib—here, indeed, are the two best models of that love of God which ought to fill our own souls !

And if it were given to us to retrace the course of centuries, and to contemplate the marvellous effects of charity, as displayed in the lives of the Saints, what a wonderful picture should we have before us ! Let us listen to St. Paul, when he says to the Romans : ' Who, then, shall separate me from the love of Christ ? Neither death, nor life, nor angels, nor principalities, nor powers, nor things present, nor things to come, nor might, nor height, nor depth, nor any other creature, shall be able to separate me from the love of God. Jesus Christ is my life. I live, yet not I, but Jesus Christ liveth in me.'

'I love Thee, O my God!' exclaims St. Augustine, 'I love thee! I desire to love Thee every day more. O, Thou fairest among the children of men, grant me, I beseech Thee, the grace to love Thee as I desire and as I ought!'

O that we could still listen to the sublime raptures of a St. Dominic, of a St. Francis of Assisi, of a St. Ignatius Loyola, of a St. Francis Xavier, of a St. Francis of Sales! And is it not the glory of us, women, that we, too, have Saints, whose love for their Divine Master was no less fervent and great?—a Mary Magdalen, an Agnes, a Cecilia, a Gertrude, a Catherine of Sienna, a Theresa? And shall we remain cold and insensible when we have before us such grand models? O let us say, with another Saint: 'O my soul, created after the image of God, redeemed by the precious Blood of Jesus Christ, thou spouse of faith, thou who hast been sanctified by the Holy Spirit, and gifted with every virtue, O love Him who has loved

thee so much; think of Him who never for-
gets thee, seek Him who seeks thee, give
thyself entirely to Him who gives Himself
entirely to thee !' (Soliloque.)

EIGHTH DAY.

ON THE LOVE OF GOD (*continued*).

'Love, and do what thou wilt.' ST. AUGUSTINE.

IT is not enough to believe that we must love God with all our heart, all our soul, and all our strength.

This love must so completely fill our whole being, that we shall end by loving nothing save in and for God, and all creatures for His sake; thus will be realised St. Augustine's beautiful words, 'Love, and do what thou wilt.'

After His resurrection, Jesus, addressing Himself to him to whom He wished to confide the care of His Church here below, said to him: 'Simon, son of John, lovest thou Me? Lovest thou Me more than these?'

Thus does the Divine Master draw a distinct line of demarcation between those who are His disciples and those who are not.

Let us imagine Him addressing these same words to us each individually: 'Dost thou love Me more than these do? Lovest thou Me more than doth the world? more than do sinners? Dost thou love Me? That is to say, does there exist between thy thoughts and My thoughts, between My judgments and thy judgments, such conformity as must necessarily exist between two hearts who love one another?'

O, can we always answer with St. Peter, 'Lord, Thou knowest that I love Thee'? Do we judge of everything with the Gospel in our hands? Our Divine Master loved a humble and hidden life; we desire to be praised and honoured. He chose poverty, we wish to be rich. Sufferings were welcomed by Him as eagerly as the limpid stream is welcomed by the parched stag, whilst we fly from them with horror. When we complain that we do not find in Holy Communion that ineffable consolation which filled the souls of the Saints, when they partook of the Eucharistic banquet, we forget that it is because our hearts are not suffi-

ciently united with the Heart of our blessed
Lord. We may admire His divine beauty,
the eloquence of His words, the sublimity of
His example; but until we have really begun
to imitate Him, we cannot say with truth :
' My God, I love Thee.'

We believe ourselves to be Christians,
we call ourselves Christians, perhaps even
we may consider ourselves to be pious and
devout; and yet our Divine Lord is but a
secondary consideration in our lives. In order
to convince ourselves of this, let us honestly
pass in review the different actions of our
day.

We wake in the morning, probably at some
late hour. Now, can we say to our Lord that
we love Him above everything, if we give
way to indolence, instead of rising in time to
accomplish our duties properly, or to assist
at the Holy Sacrifice? Or if we begin our
day without, by fervent prayer, committing
ourselves to the protection of Almighty God?
For the few hurried words we perhaps murmur with our lips, whilst our minds are
far away, cannot in truth be called prayer.

Can we say, ' My God, I love Thee,' if we follow all the caprices of our fancy; if our children are not properly cared for; if our homes are neglected; if we spend our time in frivolous reading, or in self-indulgence? Do we love God when we can pass by His house without even a thought of crossing its threshold to adore His supreme Majesty, in the tabernacle where His love lies waiting?

How can our lips dare to pronounce words of devotion and of love to the all pure and holy God, when we deck ourselves out in such a manner that we become the occasions of temptation and perhaps of sin to others? or when our thoughtless and unkind words wound and injure our neighbour?

Can we say, ' My God, I love Thee,' . when the interests of Jesus are not our interests? O, if our own self-love is wounded, if we experience some worldly loss, if sickness comes upon us, then we complain, and often bitterly; but when it is Jesus who is injured, when His sacred name is profaned, His holy day not observed, and His laws ·

violated, and all this often by those over whom we have control, then we remain cold and indifferent, and we scarcely notice it. The poor, those friends of our dear Lord, are cold and hungry; do we even know that they are suffering? and besides, what do we care?

O, how then shall we learn how we are to love God, and especially how we are to show our love? Let us once more turn our eyes upon him who watched over the Saviour's cradle with so much tenderness and devotion. Every instant of St. Joseph's life was an act of love; nothing occupied him but the care of the holy Child; he identified himself with Him, lived in His life, and suffered with Him.

But who are they, in these our days, who know how to suffer for God? And yet, as Jesus proved His love for us by His sufferings and His death, so in like manner ought we to show our own for Him by our sufferings, and by our acceptance of that sentence of death which God has pronounced against guilty man.

Besides, a soul which is really filled with divine love is so raised above itself, that to be laden with chains for the sake of Jesus Christ, and to be persecuted for Him, is its greatest glory and happiness. When the love of God really takes possession of a soul, it can effect marvels. We do not feel these truths; we do not realise them, because our hearts are tepid and icy. 'It is, O my God, not to love Thee enough to love anything else except in Thee and for Thee' (St. Augustine).

Let us, then, say with one, whose generous and noble heart had well understood the beauty of love: 'Henceforth I desire only to be known among the children of men by these words: she who believes, who prays, and who loves.' (Mdme. Swetchine.)

NINTH DAY.

ON OBEDIENCE.

'Lord, what wouldst Thou have me to do?'
St. Paul.

WHEN God created man, He created him free; but as it was His wish to give him eternal happiness, He imposed upon him a trial, in order to be able to bestow it as a recompense of his fidelity. He gave His first commandment to Adam and Eve; they disobeyed God's orders, and we know what were the fatal consequences of that first abuse of liberty; an abuse which was to be followed by so many others. Later on, God spoke to men by His prophets, until the day when the Word came down from heaven, in order not only to redeem us by His precious Blood, but to convert our fallen humanity, and to recall it to the observance of the divine laws. Before our Lord returned to heaven, He founded His Church—that company of the faithful which was to endure to the end of time, transmitting to each generation, in spite of all persecutions, the sacred treasures contained in the Gospel.

God is life and truth. Uncertainty and caprice, those two great obstacles which we meet with in the obedience we render to creatures, are never found in Him. His will is plain and easy to be understood. As a proof of our love, He demands the submission of our minds and hearts; and we know that obedience will be made easy to us by the clearness of His orders, and by the help He will give us to enable us to execute them.

The first thing, therefore, which we have to do, in order to show our love of God, is to be obedient to His commands. We know them all, and this is not the place to make a special study of them.

Besides this, the Church has received from our Lord the mission to promulgate His laws and precepts, which are no less binding

on our consciences than the ten commandments.

Are our lives really in conformity with
these divine commands ? Let us judge our
own hearts, and ask ourselves whether we
can truly call ourselves faithful disciples.
The will of God is also made known to us
through the medium of those whom God
has appointed to be our superiors, whether
in a social point of view, or in domestic life.
We shall see what is the obedience we owe
them, when we come to speak of our duty
to our neighbour.

Our lives are chequered by a number of
events, which are quite independent of our
own will. The world looks upon them as
the effects of chance; but we should see in
them the manifestation of God's will with
regard to us, for He rules and orders even
the most trifling details of our lives, and
makes them all concur in our greater good.
In this way does He providentially watch over
His creatures. Obedience means the submission of the will; and our submission must
consist in conforming ourselves, without re-

serve, to the will of God. We have, each one of us, our appointed place here below; and our misfortune is, that, not content with the lot which has been given us, we wish to become what it is not intended that we should be, and would fain cast away the trials and the sorrows which our Lord sends us for our greater perfection.

There are many persons who are most desirous of serving God, and working for His glory, who yet are often tempted by the devil in a way against which we ought to be on our guard. He tries to convince us, that if we are not pious, good, charitable, and patient, it is entirely the fault of the circumstances in which we are placed, and the persons with whom we live; and that were we in some different position, which we picture to ourselves, in our imagination, as free from all the troubles of our present state, we should easily attain to a high state of perfection. These thoughts cause us to neglect the daily efforts we ought to make, and our progress in the spiritual life is consequently slow.

We must resolutely turn away from such

dangerous thoughts. Let us remember that God only vouchsafes to us the present moment, and that we ought to make the best use of it; for death may surprise us ere we reach the particular position of which we have been dreaming.

St. Joseph's whole life and conduct offers us here an admirable example. He gives himself up unreservedly to the guidance of God, who leads him first to Bethlehem, then into Egypt, and finally to Nazareth. The will of God is the sole rule of all his actions, and he is not afraid to submit himself blindly to it.

'Let us give ourselves up to God, that He may do with us what He wills. Let there never be a single moment of voluntary resistance on our part; and whenever our evil inclinations tempt us to rebel, let us throw ourselves with confidence on God, protesting that we desire to do His bidding in spite of our own weak and corrupt nature. His holy Spirit will little by little help us to overcome and subdue it, if we will but trust in Him.

'To wish to serve God in one place rather than in another, in some certain way and in no other, is to desire to serve Him after our own liking, and not after His. But to be ready to do anything; to will everything, and yet nothing; to be as a puppet in the hands of Providence; to put no limits to our submission, since the kingdom of God has no limits—that is to serve Him, and to sacrifice ourselves; that is really to acknowledge Him to be our God, and we His creatures made only for Him. O, how happy ought we to be if, by any sufferings of our own, we could add but one degree to His glory!

'What are we good for if our hearts still refuse their entire and unreserved submission to Him who is their Maker?' (Fénélon.)

'O, Will of Him whom we love, divine Will, which, if not always understood, is yet ever known; that Will in which no injustice can be feared, and the mysteries of which we revere; O, Will most holy, of which, even to gain heaven, we dare not complain; adorable Will, the law of all created beings, the joy of the elect; blessed Will, glorifying the post which it assigns, giving strength for the sacrifice which it commands, and consolation for the sorrow which it sends!

'O, will of my God, take possession of my will, bear it away more swiftly than did the earth leave the chaos out of which it was created, or the light appeared at Thy command; more swiftly than Thy Saints forget the sorrows of this life when they come to the enjoyment of Thy heavenly kingdom.

'O, Will of my God, be thou ever my will, and until my last hour initiate me into Thy secrets, and teach me to understand more and more their hidden and ever-growing mysteries.' (Mde. Swetchine.)

TENTH DAY.

'With desolation is all the land made desolate,
because there is none that considereth in the
heart.' JER. xii. 11.

THE French nation has often been called a
frivolous nation. I should like to be able
to exonerate my country from this accusation which is made against it from all sides,
and which it seems but too willing to accept.

Let us at least inquire whether we each
individually deserve our share of this general accusation.

When long ago God commanded His prophet to warn a guilty people of the chastisements which were in store for it, He
concluded with these words: 'With desolation is all the land made desolate, because
there is none that considereth in the heart.'

How true this still is in the present day!
Yes, our lives are much too exterior; and
I am not now speaking of those women of
the world who are never satisfied unless
they are going out, and who would be quite
unhappy were they obliged to pass a single
day without receiving or paying an endless
succession of visits.

But there is a universal tendency among
us to dissipation of mind. We shrink from
recollecting ourselves, or from any kind of
reflection. Solitude fatigues and bores us.
Even women who are given up to good
works, who go about visiting the poor, and
whose names appear in every charitable as-
sociation, are themselves subject to this disastrous influence; and really interior souls
become every day more rare.

There is, I know, an excuse which we
have always ready. Solitude, we say, is
intended for those whom God has called in
an especial manner; it is the portion of a
religious life; but with all the different
duties of the mother of a family, of the
mistress of a home, and of the society in

which we are thrown, it is impossible to be otherwise.

But here is a dangerous and fatal error.

I allow that it is more difficult for us to reflect and to recollect ourselves than it is for the Carmelite, who has voluntarily separated herself from all the distractions of the world; but, on the other hand, it is more necessary. Thrown, as we are, into every sort of danger, and surrounded by the temptations of a deceitful world, we ought often to stop and reflect, and to withdraw ourselves into that secret chamber spoken of in the Gospels, and there to weigh in the balance of the sanctuary the divers elements of which our lives are composed.

Examples of this are not wanting: queens, princesses, women who by their position in life seemed called to play a conspicuous part in the world, have found time to recollect themselves before God, without neglecting the duties of their calling. And he who has been called the master of the interior life, St. Joseph, did he live under the shade of the cloister, was he separated from the

G

world by an iron grating? No; his life
was passed in the fulfilment of his domestic
duties; poverty obliged him to spend many
hours of the day in manual labour; and yet
the humble house at Nazareth was a perfect model of that religious solitude, without which the soul cannot raise herself to
God.

By solitude we mean silence, and the
avoidance of everything which is likely to
disturb our peace of mind. Without being
a hermit in the desert or in the cloister,
there is such a thing as compulsory solitude. In the midst of the pleasures and
cares which distract us, have we ever remembered the solitude of those who are in
prison? A most dismal and bitter solitude,
unless, indeed, the poor forsaken one has
appealed to our Lord to lighten his heavy
chain, and change his sufferings into inestimable blessings! How many souls have
been converted and transformed within the
four walls of a prison! Listen how Silvio
Pellico, imprisoned under the burning leads
at Venice, exclaims in the fervour of his

thankfulness : ' My sufferings are as nothing, since my solitude has taught me the
one thing necessary—religion.'

Who can tell us all the spiritual joy which
God granted to the Saints whom persecution
had thrown into dark and dismal dungeons ?
How near were they to God, in spite of all the
bolts and bars which separated them from
their fellow-men ! and how deep was their
happiness when the great Consoler, hidden
under the Eucharistic species, came to feed
and strengthen their souls ! Only the other
day did we not hear the echoes of their
voices still raised in thanksgiving in the
cells of La Roquette ?

' O prison, beloved prison ! thou whose
walls I have kissed, exclaiming, *Bona crux !*
O, how much do I not owe thee ! No longer
art thou a prison—thou art a chapel. Thou
art not even solitude, since I am not alone ;
for my Lord and my King, my Master and
my God, has deigned to dwell here with
me. It is not only in thought that I draw
near to Him ; He does not merely infuse
His grace into my heart, but really and cor-

porally did He come to visit and console
me, His poor prisoner, and remain with me;
He wills to do this, and can He not do it,
since He is omnipotent ?' ' O blessed cap-
tivity, mayest thou last for ever ! For art
thou not the means of my bearing my God
in my heart, not as a sign, but in the reality of my living union with Him ?' (Le
P. Clerc.)

Then there is the solitude of the sick.
We must have felt it, in order to understand it thoroughly. It is a necessity of
their state; but it is no less wearisome to
nature, until we can realise that a bed of
sickness is a cross upon which God has
bound us; then such solitude is profitable;
and when danger warns us of that decree
of death, of which the Apostle speaks, and
which we all bear within us, then do we
learn to appreciate things at their true
value. By the light of faith our souls at
last see the futility of all the things of this
world, and the hope of heaven soothes our
sufferings and reanimates our courage.

Solitude is the right preparation for all

that is serious and great. The philosopher requires it for his labour; the artist for the conception of his works; the general to prepare his plan of battle. The very silence of the night precedes and seems given as a preparation for the splendours of the coming day; so much the more necessary then is solitude for us, in order to enable us to accomplish the work of our salvation.

In thus advocating the practice of silence and recollection, it must, of course, be well understood that we are not to employ our solitude in allowing our minds to build *castles in the air*, nor indulge ourselves in dreams of the imagination, which leave behind them nothing but ennui, sadness, and discouragement.

Let us have our hour's, or at least our quarter of an hour's solitude; but let us not spend it in vague and idle thoughts, which only become a snare to us.

As the labourer in the fields, tired by his long and continued work, and exhausted by the heat of the burning sun, leaves for a moment the field where he is reaping, and seeks some repose beneath the trees of the road-side, in order to return again to his labour with more strength and courage; so should we, from time to time, retire from the turmoil of the world, and go and repose ourselves at the feet of our Lord. This repose is not yet prayer, but it is the first and most indispensable condition of it. God does not let Himself be heard in the soul in the midst of the bustle of the world. He leads her into solitude, and then, as the Scriptures tell us, He speaks to her heart to heart.

ELEVENTH DAY.

ON PRAYER (*continued*).

'Whatsoever you shall ask the Father in My name, that will I do.' ST. JOHN.

MAN is miserably poor. God is the source of all good.

Man is guilty. God is His judge.

Such is our position before God. But we must add that the Sovereign Master has but one desire—that of enriching His creatures; and that the God we have offended seeks but one thing—to pardon the guilty.

On what condition, then, will the liberality and mercy of God be exercised towards us? On one condition alone, which is clearly expressed by our Divine Master: ' Whatsoever you shall ask the Father in My name, that will I do.' (St. John.) To ask, is to pray.

Prayer is the great want of our hearts. It is the raising of our souls to God. It is a word, a cry, a sigh, a look, a tear, even silence, provided it springs from the heart and says, ' My God !'

As prayer is the act of a heart which pleads, we must, in order to receive what we ask for, enter into ourselves with a spirit of recollection. As we said yesterday, a dissipated mind cannot pray, or at least, cannot pray with fruit.

Let us listen to our Saviour's words : not only He teaches us how to pray in the Gospel, but He points out to us likewise the dispositions which we should bring when we pray. Each word that falls from the Saviour's lips is full of strength, life, and light.

' Thou, when thou shalt pray, enter into thy chamber, and having shut the door, pray to thy Father in secret.' (St. Matthew vi. 6.)

We must, therefore, first separate ourselves from all the things of this world, leave them on one side, raise ourselves above them. It is but too true that we may be outwardly recollected, and place ourselves in the darkest corner of the church, or the quietest part of our own house, and yet be inwardly distracted. How often, alas, have we not been startled and surprised, even at the foot of the altar, at finding our thoughts preoccupied by the wretched cares or anxieties of life, from which we have such trouble in freeing ourselves !

Is, then, attention, the concentration of all our faculties on any one subject, so very difficult to us ? We cannot say that we are incapable of it. Have we never been entirely engrossed by the dangers of a relative or friend, by the probable issue of some important affair, and (who knows ?) by something in which our own self-love or interest was concerned, and which so absorbed our minds as to make us almost unconscious of what was going on around us ? Well, it is thus we must be before our Lord, if we would really *pray*.

What is our object when we kneel down to perform that essential duty of the life of every Christian? To render, first, homage and praise to God as our Sovereign Master.

Let us pause for a moment on this thought, and try to recollect ourselves. Do we fulfil, as we should, this first important object in prayer—I mean thankfulness? We feel the need of having recourse to God in our necessities; but do we remember to thank Him for all that He has done for us, His poor and unworthy creatures? I fear that this first part of the duty of prayer is too often neglected. Yet if we read the Psalms, which are such models of devotion, we shall see in what eloquent accents the Prophet-King praises the greatness of God, and exalts His mercy.

The second object of prayer is to bring our daily wants and needs before God. Here we might feel that our own interests were in question; but we must take care to understand clearly what is meant by our daily wants.

The pagans prayed to their gods; but it was for material things, for riches, for honours, and even for the means of satisfying their passions.

We are Christians; and although we may
be tempted to ask of God temporal rather
than spiritual blessings, yet our desires
should go beyond this fleeting life; for when
our Lord says in the Gospel, 'Ask, and ye
shall receive,' He means principally *spiritual*
graces.

Our Saviour Himself has given us a model
of prayer; and I would it were given to me
to meditate here on each of the admirable
petitions contained in the *Pater Noster*.
But I will only remark in passing that *one
only* relates to temporal things : ' *Give us
this day our daily bread.*' Not opulence, not
even ordinary comfort, is implied in these
words, but simply what is necessary for the
preservation of life, and even that we only
ask for day by day.   What a lesson !

We often complain of being unable to
resist temptation.   Have we as often thought
of asking God to give us strength, and patience, and gentleness, and submission ? Ah,
if the Saints were all-powerful with God, it
was because they knew how to pray and
what to ask for.   They did not waste their

time in useless supplications for things of
this world. Of course, we are not forbidden
to lay our temporal wants before our Lord,
and to ask Him to cause our earthly business to prosper, if it be His will. But what
I mean is, that such petitions must be secondary.

Let us remember the example set us by
Solomon. God, in His mercy and goodness, asks him what it is he wishes for most.
And what is his reply? Not honours or
riches, but *wisdom;* and we all know how
his desire was granted.

Let us remember that we must seek *first*
the kingdom of God and His justice, and
that all the rest will be added to us.

Again, when we speak to God of those we
love, let our intentions be raised above this
earthly scene. Let us ask for them, before
everything else, the precious gift of grace,
that they may obtain eternal salvation.

Let us never forget that our prayers
will be worthless before God, unless offered
through the merits of our Divine Redeemer.
' Whatsoever you shall ask the Father in

My name, that will I do.' Jesus has made Himself our intercessor before God the Father, our advocate, the defender of our interests; but then we must plead in His name.

Ah, if we did but know the power of such prayers, how rapidly we should progress in virtue! How many souls would be saved!

Our Lord often tries our faith. He does not grant our petitions at once. Perseverance, in fact, is one of the conditions of prayer. That which we beseech of God in the spiritual order is of countless price. We cannot plead too earnestly or with too much persistence. 'Ask, and it shall be given you; seek, and you shall find; knock, and it shall be opened to you.' Never let us weary of thus pleading before our Lord, with all the confidence of souls that know that He to whom we address ourselves is as good as He is powerful. Let us try and picture to ourselves the three persons of the Holy Family, prostrate in the presence of God. How eloquent must they have been when their voices were raised to heaven to praise the Divine Majesty, and to plead with Him for the salvation of the world !

May we strive to realise, with Jesus, Mary, and Joseph, the power of intercessory prayer in days like these, when the divine justice seems on the point of falling on a guilty world, and when such pleading alone may avail to stop His avenging arm !

TWELFTH DAY.

ON PRAYER (*continued*).

'Pray without ceasing.' ST. LUKE.

PRAYER, that is the raising of our soul towards God, is one of the most essential conditions of the Christian life. We must pray: that we have sufficiently proved in the preceding meditation. When are we to pray? 'Without ceasing' is the answer of our Divine Lord in the Gospel, wherein He spake less of a distinct act than of an habitual state of mind.

The Christian who is in that disposition of heart and mind will have recourse to God on every occasion in life. Have we not often watched a little child trying to walk for the first time? If it stumbles, if anything which it fancies is a danger comes in its way, it calls to its mother, it holds up its little hands towards her. Well, these are

the dispositions which God expects from us,
—a confidence, a certainty of being heard,
and of our prayer being granted.

Prayer is a duty. We thus render to
God the homage which is His due, and He
who is the Sovereign Master of all things
tells us, by the voice of Holy Scripture and
by the teaching of His Church, how we can
best honour and glorify Him. Our material
life is regulated by certain laws. We have
a fixed time for sleep, for meals, for work,
for rest. In the same way, in our spiritual
life all should be in order. Even the ancients
had, like the Christians, fixed hours and days
specially consecrated to the great duty of
prayer.

David in the Psalms exclaims to his
Maker, ' Seven times a day do I praise Thee,'
and the Divine Office, which, in the first
centuries, was sung by all Christians, is also
divided into seven parts. Night and day,
certain hours were set apart for prayer. The
Apostolic Constitutions ordered the faithful
to pray in the morning at three o'clock, then
at six, at nine in the evening, and at mid-

night. We find in the writings of St. Jerome the advice given by him to Santa Paula, a noble Roman lady, on the education of her daughter.

'Put about her,' he says, 'a woman of a certain age, full of faith and modesty; let her learn from her example to rise in the night and chant the Psalms ; in the morning, sacred hymns and lessons ; and so on, at Tierce, Sext, and None; so as to live in the continual presence of Jesus Christ, and be ready courageously to fight His battles. Then towards sunset, let her pray again, lighting her lamp, like the wise virgin, to offer the evening sacrifice.'

In another of his letters, the same Saint tells us that the Christian harvesters cheered their toil by singing Psalms; while the vine-dressers, while pruning their vines, repeated the Canticles.

The majority of the faithful, in fact, in those days followed this holy custom.

' My brethren,' speaks St. Augustine, in preaching to his flock, ' try, I beseech you, to rise earlier to assist at the vigils of the

Church. Above all, never neglect the offices of Tierce, Sext, and None. Let no one be exempt from this holy practice, unless he be prevented by illness, by any public service, or by some great necessity.'

Since those days the Church, taking pity on our weakness, permitted several modifications of this rule. The precept of prayer, however, is not thereby changed; only the manner of exercising it.

But only think of the immeasurable distance which separates the fervour of the first Christians from our own idleness and spiritual tepidity. If one of us was known to rise in the middle of the night to pray, not three times, as in the first centuries of the Church, but only for the space of a quarter of an hour, what astonishment would it not create! And (why should we not say it?) what bitter ridicule would be excited by such a revelation! 'She wants to be singular,' one will say. 'She is ruining her health,' another will exclaim (although they would say nothing if she were out all night at balls); 'one must go with the times.' 'Such conduct is

foolish and extravagant.' 'She is an enthu-
siast,' &c. Granted. If the Gospel has
not been altered, our poor humanity has become so weakened in these degenerate days,
that we must have uninterrupted sleep and
a softer easier life. What can we do then,
in a religious point of view, which shall not
compromise our precious health? Let us
only think to-day of the particular duties
which each of us can perform. We do not
propose anything extraordinary or out of the
way. But let us follow in imagination our
holy Patriarch in his pious relations with
his Divine Son. At daybreak, what happiness it must have been to him to find himself near Him! Ought not our first thought
likewise to be for God? To raise our hearts
to His throne; to praise and give Him
thanks; to offer to Him the actions of the
day; to ask for His help and strength in our
work and in our struggles; to implore His
blessing on ourselves and on all whom we
love,—this should be our daily morning
prayer. Let us turn again in thought to
Joseph, conversing with Jesus on the great

mysteries of the Faith. Listen to the questions and answers of the Holy Child, and then let us strive to imitate this great master of the interior life. I do not think that any woman, who really wishes to lead a Christian life, can be excused from consecrating a quarter of an hour of each day to the holy exercise of meditation, an exercise so easy to the heart that loves God.

Would a whole day ever pass in the Holy Family without some pious intercourse? And on how many occasions during the day will not a holy woman lift up her heart to God? A fervent invocation before her work; an earnest look upwards in moments of difficulty, pain, trial, or temptation; a moment of recollection before and after meals; during the day, some instants given to reading a good book—the life of a Saint—or something that speaks to her of God: each and all of these acts come naturally to a loving heart, living in the continual realisation of His presence. Do not let us forget, either, the Rosary, that holy practice so dear to pious souls.

Then, each evening, recollecting ourselves before Him who has deigned to preserve us for another day, and add one more to those He has already granted to us, let us go over in our minds the many blessings which we owe to His mercy and goodness. Let us ask His forgiveness for our many sins and shortcomings, let us pray for the living and the dead, above all, for those in their last agony. And let us not dream of lying down to rest until we have committed our souls unto His care, who has created them for His glory.

THIRTEENTH DAY.

ON PRAYER (*continued*).

'Where there are two or three gathered together
in My name, there am I in the midst of them.'
ST. MATT. xviii. 20.

ALL religions have their exterior worship,
their temples, their altars, their place of
meeting, and their formulas of prayer and
praise.

'To deny the usefulness of rites and cere-
monies in matters of religion,' says Por-
talis, 'is to prove our own madness and
folly; for it is to deny the influence of outward forms on beings who are not pure
spirits.'

'Never let us forget,' writes Nicolas, in
his *Etudes Philosophiques*, 'that religion
should unite men among themselves by the
same link that unites them to God. It must
take possession of every part of humanity,

to consume it in the divine unity. For this purpose, it must be clothed with external and tangible forms, which unite men among themselves, and act on them collectively as well as individually.'

God is our father, and we all are brethren. What then can be more natural than to gather together round His throne, to offer Him our prayers and praise, and to tell Him of our wants? The Church is a family; and have we not often felt this at the very bottom of our hearts, when we mingle our voices with the multitude who are singing the praises of our God? Have we not often experienced the closeness and strength of this Christian union, especially in times of great public calamity? A cruel epidemic ravages a city, or a terrible hostile host is advancing towards our gates. Then we strive to realise the full meaning of our Saviour's words: 'Where there are two or three gathered together in My name, there am I in the midst of them.'

Yes, He is indeed in the midst of us—He who, by a series of miracles, has made Himself the guest of His creature; He who every day renews on the altar the tremendous sacrifice of Calvary. But, O, the ingratitude of men! Are not our churches very often almost deserted during the celebration of the holy Mysteries?

'If this most holy Sacrament were celebrated in one place only,' writes the author of the *Imitation*, 'and consecrated by only one priest in the world, with how great a desire, thinkest thou, would men be affected towards that place and to such a priest of God, that they might see the divine mysteries celebrated? But now that there are many priests, and Christ is offered up in many places, that the grace and love of God to man may appear so much the greater, by how much more bounteously is this Sacred Communion distributed throughout the entire world!'

How is it possible, in fact, for souls who have the gift of faith to absent themselves without sufficient reason from the daily attendance at Holy Mass? To a great many women, it only requires a little effort to over-

come their natural sleepiness or self-indulgence, which prevents their rising in the
morning in time to seek, at the foot of the
altar, those graces which they so greatly
need for the accomplishment of their duties.
Let us quote the words of a woman living in
the world, Mdme. de Lamartine (whose
Mémoirs have just appeared simultaneously
in French and in English), and one whom
no one can accuse of too much asceticism.
She writes in her Journal : ' I have adopted
the habit this year of going to church every
morning at dawn to hear Mass. It seems
to me that we ought to devote the first-fruits
of our day to God, before we are engrossed
by the cares and worries and pleasures of
the world; so that we may render first to
God what is due to Him, and then to the
world what it requires. I find it sometimes
a great effort to go out in all weathers, and
to leave my comfortable bed and the warm
temperature of my room, to go to what is
called here the poor people's or servants'
Mass. But are we not all poor enough in
the grace of God? and the servants of our

fathers, our husbands, our children? I feel
myself thoroughly rewarded a little later by
the spirit of recollection which I feel in this
half-light, by the greater fervour of my prayers, and by the calm and strength which I
gain for the rest of the day, through the feeling of the presence of God and the thought
of my first great duty having been accomplished.'

There are not only fixed hours for prayer,
there are also certain days set apart for that
purpose.   All our moments belong to God ;
but He has left us a special commandment
for the sanctification of the seventh day.
Holy Scripture tells us of the admirable
manner in which the Sabbath was observed
under the old law.   The Holy Family is in
this respect, as in all others, the best model
for our imitation.

But this law, delivered by God Himself
in the Old Testament, and promulgated anew
by our Divine Master in the Gospels, is unfortunately too much neglected in these days.
Its violation is certainly one of the causes of
the terrible chastisements which have befal-

len our country. Let us then, as Christian women, unite our efforts for this one end—that of causing this great day to be observed by all those who are placed under our authority, servants, workmen, artisans, &c. It is not enough to abstain on Sundays from any manual or servile work ourselves; we must try to spare our servants as much as we can, so as to enable them to perform their religious duties; for the Lord's day should be consecrated specially to His service, and that we too often forget.

I should like to quote here the whole of a beautiful conference on this subject by Monseigneur le Courtier, entitled *Le Dimanche des Femmes* (Retraite Annuelle des Dames, p. 173). I earnestly beg my readers to get it for themselves.

There are regular services in all our parish churches, and we excuse ourselves from assisting at them, and very often without sufficient reason. The word of God is preached to us at High Mass, and many Sundays pass without our even thinking of attending it. The hours devoted to vespers, sermon, and benediction in the afternoon are continually spent by us in frivolous reading, talking, or paying and receiving visits, and so on, all through the day. Let us then, once for all, understand the obligation which is laid upon every Christian to keep holy the Sabbath day. It is our reproach, as Catholics, that we do not observe it as the Protestants do. But, without falling into their errors of judaic and gloomy observance, are we not equally bound to spend at least the largest portion of it in the sanctification of our own souls? Let us watch over our children and servants, taking care that nothing shall hinder them in their religious duties.*

---

* I know of one lady, herself a great invalid, who will not allow a fire to be lit in her bedroom on Saturday evenings, even in the coldest weather, lest the cleaning of the grate should cause her housemaid to miss Sunday morning's Mass. Most of our faults arise from want of thought. So ladies take their carriages out on Sunday morning even when the church is near at hand ; thereby preventing their coachman from having a chance of attending to his duties. Yet, in the great day of account, shall we not be held responsible for such things?

Holy Scripture tells us that, on one occasion, God having been consulted as to the punishment to be inflicted on a man who had gathered wood on the Sabbath day, He ordered him to be stoned.

I stop here, and leave this instance to your serious meditation.

FOURTEENTH DAY.

BETHLEHEM AND THE ALTAR.

'My delight is to be with the children of men.'
PROVERBS.

IF we were to reduce the Catholic faith to that which constitutes its essential part, we should find nothing more simple, nothing which lends itself so much to extreme poverty of outward circumstances. A little bread, a little wine, a few words spoken by the mouth of a Priest—there is all the Sacrifice of the Mass! which yet is the highest expression of divine worship, as it is the most admirable *résumé* of it.

'A stone, a dungeon, a barn, a grotto, a wooded dell—each and all may become an Altar and a Temple for Him who had not even a stone on which to lay His head, and who sanctifies all things by His presence.' (Nicolas.)

It is now nearly nineteen centuries ago that the shepherds and the Magi came to render their homage of prayer and praise to the God who dwells in our tabernacles. The temple where the Divine Majesty then deigned to dwell, under the semblance of a little child, was the humble stable of Bethlehem—the poor grotto of the Nativity. Mary's lap was the throne of the incarnate God; and Joseph, that model of priests, offered Him their adoration.

In meditating on the adorable mysteries which were accomplished in the cradle of Jesus, we have often been tempted to envy those happy shepherds, to whom the angels gave notice of the birth of the Messiah; or those Magi, who were guided by the miraculous star to the very feet of the holy Child. Ah, how gladly would we also have offered Him presents, had one glance from the Saviour, one word from Mary, some little encouragement from Joseph! But why should we envy a happiness which we can share? The veil under which Jesus is hidden is thicker, but the reality is the same. The

Altar is Bethlehem. Jesus as a Child—Jesus as the sacred Host—to the eye of faith, where is the difference? Between what He granted to St. Joseph and what He gives to us, the advantage is really on our side.

It seems, at first sight, impossible to imagine a more intimate union than that which existed between Jesus and Joseph, and yet our glorious Patriarch never had the happiness of Communion. He held the infant God in his arms, it is true. But never had he the happiness of partaking of the Eucharistic Banquet, where the Saviour Himself makes Himself our food.

We therefore have nothing to envy him on that score. But let us compare, if we dare, our coldness with his love; our distractions before the Altar, our indifference even for Holy Communion, with the fervour and the zeal which burnt in his heart! Jesus had been born poor; Joseph and Mary, by their efforts and by their daily toil, strove to make His childhood less full of sufferings and privations. With what love did not Mary spin and weave the linen which was

to clothe her Divine Son! If we had been
allowed to share in this holy occupation,
with what joy should we have performed
the task !

Let us console ourselves with this thought.
Jesus, dwelling as He does amongst us,
wishes to remain poor; and deigns to accept
our offerings as of old He accepted the offerings of the Magi and the humble toil of Mary.

We too need gold for our churches, and
incense, and myrrh, and fine linen, to receive
that sacred Host, 'without stain or blemish,'
whom we adore on our Altars.

Have not our hearts often beat painfully
at the sight of the utter poverty of poor
country churches? Listen to a pious exhor-
tation addressed by Mgr. Dupanloup, the
illustrious Bishop of Orleans, to Christian
women on this subject :

' I have seen Protestants—who do not believe in the Real Presence, but who yet know
that it is an article of our faith—stand aghast
at the sight of our dishonoured altars ; of our
miserable sanctuaries ; of our Communion-
tables, falling to pieces from age ; of our tar-

nished chalices and other sacred vessels, destined to carry Extreme Unction to the sick,
yet in the most disgraceful state ; sacristies
so damp as to be positively unwholesome, and
threatening to corrupt that which is the most
sacred of all things here below. And then
the tabernacles, where the living God deigns
to dwell !   I have seen some where a worldly
woman would not for a moment leave her fine
things . . . . . Eternal King of all the earth,
is this the way Thou art treated?   Ah, it is
not needful to have a priest's heart; it is
enough to be a Christian to blush and grieve
at such a fearful scandal.   As for me, I cannot resign myself to such a sad state of things,
and I own I have a difficulty in comprehending the resignation of certain people, who
quietly go to Communion week after week,
and receive the Benediction of the Blessed
Sacrament day after day, and yet never dream
of making the smallest sacrifice to remedy
so disgraceful a neglect.

' There is no doubt that you occupy your-
selves in a multitude of good works with great
zeal—works which plead for you before God

and are your glory; but I do not hesitate to say that, next to the work of the seminaries, which gives you priests, the work of which I am speaking, the care of the tabernacles, is the first and most important; and that nothing ought to call forth greater efforts and zeal on your part.'

Let us, then, think seriously of our duties in this respect. Let us sacrifice our superfluities—employ gold, rich silk stuffs, beautiful lace, not for the adornment of our own persons, but for the decoration of God's altar. Let our hands be occupied in making vestments, which may serve for the celebration of the Holy Mysteries; in hemming the linen cloths which are to touch the Sacred Body of Jesus Christ, and will be impregnated with His precious Blood. There is, besides, such a consolation, such a happiness in working for Him who has so loved us! O, how much a woman is to be pitied who does not understand such an enjoyment!

In the days of faith, the great of the earth considered it the highest honour to occupy themselves with all that concerned the Holy

Eucharist. The Emperor Constantine did
not consider it inconsistent with his dignity
to carry the materials destined for the building
of a church. St. Wenceslas, king of Bohe-
mia, sowed the wheat of which the consecrated
bread was made, and himself prepared the
wine for the sacrifice. St. Helena built a
multitude of churches. St. Margaret, queen
of Scotland, devoted herself to the decoration
of the altars. St. Matilda sent the imperial
robes of her son to the church of St. Martin
of Tours. The Blessed Frances d'Amboise
devoted long hours to making the sacred
linen. St. Elizabeth of Hungary offered her
wedding-gown on the altar. The same living and ardent faith animated Madame
Swetchine when she employed all her jewels
in the adornment of the sanctuary.

Let us follow these touching examples.
Let gold, silk, lace, and linen be transformed
in our hands into fresh ornaments for divine worship; let us bring flowers, make
nosegays, weave garlands; do all in our
power worthily to decorate His altars, who
deigns to dwell on them for our sakes; above

all, let us bring to this holy work all that taste, luxury, refinement, and delicacy, which women of the world know so well how to employ when it is a question of adorning their own persons. And then we shall emulate the example of Mary and of Joseph, and like the Magi, bring our offerings likewise to the Holy Child.

FIFTEENTH DAY.

ON DETACHMENT.

'Those souls only fly towards God who do not, as
it were, touch the earth, because there is nothing
that they desire there.' St. Gregory.

THE spirit of the world is opposed to the
Spirit of God; and every step that we take
in the knowledge of religious truth demon-
strates this to us more forcibly. Men say,
in their folly, ' Happy are the rich ! Happy
are those who, with their gold, can purchase for themselves a variety of enjoyments;
for to enjoy is to live. To-morrow we die ;
let us crown ourselves with roses before they
fade.'

But our Saviour Jesus Christ, who is come
to bring us eternal blessings, says, with
supreme authority, 'Blessed are the poor !'
How strange those words sound to those who
have not penetrated the secrets of faith !

Poor! Can we think, even, without terror of the loss of our fortunes? These comforts, which have become so necessary to us; this refined luxury, these useless objects, which seem to us so indispensable,—O, how we cling to them all! How impossible it would seem to us to be happy without them! We cannot even imagine that any other kind of existence is possible to us; and if, by one of those catastrophes which are so common in these days of revolution and anarchy, one of our friends happens to fall from his high social position to a mediocrity which would, after all, confer happiness on many others, we pity him with all our hearts, we think nothing is to be compared to his misfortunes. Now, in following out this train of thought, I do not mean to say that we should renounce all our fortune to serve God. The early Christians, it is true, sold their goods, and brought the produce to the Apostles to distribute to the poor, while they lived themselves in a thorough spirit of detachment from this world's treasures. But the times are changed, and God does not require of

Christians in this nineteenth century the sacrifices which were joyfully made in the first
ages of the Church.   But there is one thing
which never varies, and that is the spirit of
the Gospel, and the words of our Lord,
' Blessed are the poor!'   They are as true
now as on the day when they were spoken.

God has lent to us the goods of this world,
but He has given us nothing; and the day
is not far off when He will have everything
back. To-day this house, this château, these
woods, these fields, these jewels, are ours;
to-morrow they will belong to others—our
heirs; our days pass like smoke, and vanish
like swift running water, of which one cannot
stop the flow.   In a very short time people
will pass where I was, and will not find me.
' This was her room, this was her bed,' they
will say; and of all this nothing will remain
but my tomb, where people will say I am;
but I shall not be even there. (Bossuet.)

' The whole of our life is spent in preparing to live. We wish to make our home
perfect; we arrange our house with the utmost care; " only one thing more," and then

nothing will be wanting. It seems as if each day everything must be completed, that to-morrow we shall go in and settle; and the end of life comes before we are yet installed. In truth, this world is but an inn, where we are to sojourn for a night. What does it signify what kind of lodging we find? or what place we are to occupy? Of what use is it to give ourselves so much trouble and worry to have it a little larger, or a little more beautiful, when we can only keep it for such a very short time? What a height of folly it is to spend so many hours in making a bed for our last moments, where perhaps, after all, we shall not be able to lie! Where is the madman, who, having only a night to spend in a certain spot, begins to collect stones to build himself a palace? The length of our life answers as little to the extent of our plans for the future as does this madman's dream of a night. Are we not always well enough lodged to be ready for a start? Courage! It is only for a night. The stars are already far advanced in their course; the day is at hand!' (Alfred Tonnelle).

A true Christian spirit enables us to look upon fortune, honours, pleasures, and the like, as simply a detail of existence. The word of God is clear : ' Blessed are the poor in spirit, for theirs is the kingdom of heaven;' and, as we have said before, our Lord has joined example to instruction.

He came down from heaven the King of kings, the Lord and Master of all created things. We might have thought that He would have chosen a palace to surpass in magnificence all the riches of the East ; that richly dressed courtiers would surround His throne; that His Mother would be one of the greatest queens on earth ; and that to him to whom He granted the title of father would be given incalculable treasures. But no ; the stable of Bethlehem ; the workshop of Nazareth; the daily toil of Joseph, gaining the daily bread of the Saviour by the sweat of his brow; the privations of the public life of Jesus, during which He could say, ' The birds of the air have nests, and the foxes have holes, but the Son of Man has not where to lay His head;' His very coat, for which they cast lots at the foot of the Cross;—behold our Master's choice, and study well the lot He preferred before all others! In the same way as the poor shepherds were the first round the cradle, so the Apostles were all poor men. His disciples became so from choice; and even now those who wish to follow nearest to Him voluntarily renounce the goods of this world; while Jesus warns us that, so far from being an advantage, riches are an obstacle to our eternal salvation. Woe to the rich! Alas, the spirit of the world is still living in us so vividly that it requires a real effort on our part to judge of things by our Lord's standard. In principle we admit these truths, the evidence of which we cannot deny; but we esteem the transitory riches of this life far beyond their real value, forgetting that they are to many the cause of extreme peril, if not of eternal perdition.

Even in our judgments of others, the fact of people being rich or not, does it not greatly influence our opinion? 'She is very rich,' we say of a woman, with a kind of admira-

tion, as if that entitled her to a special amount
of respect and consideration. In the same
way, we think it an exceptional case if we
find a beautiful and noble soul among persons deprived of position or worldly riches;
forgetting that in the eyes of God the poor
are more than the rich, and that our servants,
whom we look upon as our inferiors, and
whom, perhaps, we treat with haughtiness
and disdain, are often nearer to our Lord
than we are, and have one less obstacle between Him and them!

To sum up all we have been saying in a
few words: the world places the rich man
on the highest rung of the social ladder, and
Jesus promises His kingdom to the poor.
He who overthrows empires and casts down
the monarchs of the earth from their thrones,
even when they think themselves the most
securely seated, has prepared for His elect,
not a transitory kingdom, not a throne
which will crumble away, but an eternal
mansion in the heavens. Lazarus will reign
in the bosom of God, while Dives will lift up
his eyes in hell, being in torments.

SIXTEENTH DAY.

ON THE PRESENCE OF GOD.

'All the days of thy life have God in thy mind.'
TOBIAS iv. 6.

IT is only in eternity that we shall see God face to face. Until that solemn hour when shadows will give place to reality, the material part of our being will, as we have seen in speaking of faith, be a sort of wall between our souls and the clear vision of God. But if we do not see God, we are not the less certain that we are continually in His presence. In Him we have our life and being; and if for one single instant He were to abandon us, we should return into the nothingness out of which we were taken. And His power, thus continually exercised over His creatures, constitutes, in fact, that wise and good Providence, which is one of His most perfect attributes.

If we cannot see God, we are called upon
to contemplate His works every day and
every minute of our lives. 'God,' says St.
Thomas, 'has imprinted in visible characters
upon us, His creatures, made in His image,
that which exists in Him as in an imma-
terial spirit;' and it is in this sense that we
may see here below the fulfilment of those
words of our Blessed Lord, 'Blessed are
the clean of heart, for they shall see God.'

The first feeling produced in our souls by
the thought of the presence of God and His
continual influence over our hearts, is a feeling of gratitude. For, as St. Augustine
tells us, ' He watches over each one of us,
day and night, with as much solicitude as
if we were the only creatures to be cared
for, either in heaven or on earth.'

The Lord said to Abraham, 'Walk before Me, and be perfect,' and the royal Prophet, speaking of the causes of the sinner's
iniquities, says, ' There is no fear of God
before his eyes, for in His sight he hath
done deceitfully.' And the same thought is
thus expressed by St. Augustine, ' If thou

wouldst commit evil, seek out a place where
God will not see thee, and then do what
thou wilt!' But this place, where shall we
find it? 'If I ascend into heaven, Lord,'
says the Psalmist, 'Thou art there; if I
descend into hell, Thou art present. Whither shall I go from Thy spirit, or whither
shall I flee from Thy face? And I said, Perhaps darkness shall cover me, and night
shall be light as the day. The darkness
thereof, and the light thereof, are alike to
Thee.'

Could we, indeed, find a more powerful motive to curb our passions than this thought:
' He, whom I am about to offend; He, who is
my God, my Creator, my Father; He, who
will be my judge, is now here present; it is
before Him that I am going to commit this
sin'? And the Scripture has expressed the
sinner's misery by these words, full of sadness : 'He has forgotten God.' Forgetfulness of God! Can we imagine a more
terrible misfortune? God is not only the
witness of human actions; but He who rules

the world is also the scrutiniser of our intentions.

Men do not really know each other, and we do not know ourselves.

It is only our words, our actions, our exterior acts, which can be known and judged of by our fellow-men; but the inner sanctuary of our hearts, who can penetrate sufficiently into its depths to discover all its secrets? How many troubles, how many different impressions, how many storms, agitate and upset our souls, even when our faces reveal nothing to those around us of the tempest which rages within?

God alone knows His own creature. We are before Him like an open book; nothing escapes Him; and this thought, dreadful as it is to the sinner, must surely be one full of supreme comfort to the Christian. He whom we love, our Saviour, our only Friend in the full meaning of the word, He understands us truly; and each one of our thoughts, each one of our sufferings, is weighed by Him according to its real value. He gives us grace for every trial, a reward for every sacrifice; neither will He forget anything on that day when all the troubles and bitternesses of this life will be changed into ineffable joys.   O, why do we not, then, let this truth sink deep into our hearts?   We should find in it a balm for every wound, and under its influence the saddest and the most joyless lives would soon change their aspect. 'My soul was troubled within myself; then I remembered the presence of my God, and my heart was filled with joy.'

SEVENTEENTH DAY.

'For our time is as the passing of a shadow, and
there is no going back of our end : for it is fast
sealed, and no man returneth.' WISDOM xi. 5.

WE have seen that Almighty God only
lends us the goods of this world. The time
too which He has placed at our disposition
belongs to us no more than do riches or
pleasures ; our very impossibility to stop its
march proves the truth of this.

How are we to define time? An imperceptible point between two eternities. The
moment in which I am speaking is already
gone for ever. 'An hour strikes, we count
the hours only after they are lost.' (Young.)

Gold is less precious than time; the former can but procure for us the goods of this
world, whilst the latter is the coin with

which we may purchase eternity. Are we
not, then, most foolish? We treasure up our
gold; we think we have done a meritorious
action if we give away a few pieces of it;
and we throw away our time without the
smallest compunction, heedlessly giving it to
whoever asks for it, and often to those who
have no right to it. We have too much
time; we don't know what to do with it;
hence the expression, so often used to show
what our feelings are with regard to this
precious gift, *to kill time.* 'One would imagine we were speaking of some universal
enemy to the human race, against which all
mankind had combined to conspire. Life
would seem but one continual endeavour to
get rid of it. Those men are esteemed the
happiest who the least appear to feel its
weight and duration; and the great charm
both of frivolous pleasures and of serious
occupations appears to be that they shorten
the length of the days and minutes, and
seem to rid us of them almost without our
being ourselves aware that they have passed
away.' (Massillon.)

Time is a treasure, but it weighs upon us; it gives us a feeling of weariness, and we are bored by it. Yet there will come a moment when we shall in vain wish to recall the days, the hours, and the minutes which we have so recklessly thrown away on our frivolities and follies. They will not be granted to us; there will be no longer time. Eternity is beginning for us, and perhaps our hands will be empty.

We have still faith enough to turn with horror from the thought that we might lose and throw away all that the Precious Blood of our Divine Lord has purchased for us on the Cross. Well, then, let us here pause and dwell upon a thought most calculated to teach us the value of time. After any one of our sins God might call us to Himself, and then and there pass judgment on our guilty souls. And if, after our iniquities, time for expiation is still vouchsafed to us, it is because our Saviour has redeemed these days by the merits of His sufferings and of His death, so that every minute is, so to say, dyed with a drop of the Precious Blood.

We always judge of the beauty and the valuable qualities of any object by the price it has cost; let us therefore reflect how the Christian ought to esteem the hours he so often thinks so long and heavy. To lose our time is to despise our Saviour's Precious Blood.

And however long time may appear to us, it is yet so short! Men pass away like the flowers which bloom in the morning and at night are faded and trodden under foot. Generations flow on like the waves of a rapid river. Nothing can stop time, which bears after it all that seems most immovable.

'We are forced to go on, to run, such is the rapidity of the passing years; and when from time to time we would fain make a halt, we are ever pressed forward, onwards, and onwards. And yet we see the past crumble to pieces behind us; nothing but ruin and destruction. We console ourselves, because in passing along we have gathered a few flowers, a little fruit; but before the night comes, the flowers fade in our hands, and

the fruit disappears whilst we are tasting it.'
(Bossuet.)

When in the country we want to judge of
the road along which we have been walking,
we turn round and look at it. Let us do the
same now. To old age, childhood, youth,
manhood, all seems but as yesterday. It
has vanished as a watch in the night. To
each one of us God has allotted a task to be
accomplished, and He has given us the time
necessary to perform it in. Each one of our
days must be full before Him; to lose one
single hour of them is an irreparable loss;
for to no one shall it be given to redeem the
time that is lost.

It is related of Titus, that if the evening
came without his having been able to perform some good action, he wept, saying, ' I
have lost my day !'

But how are we properly to employ every
moment of our life? By the accomplishment of the will of God in us; by faithful-
ness in our Christian as well as in our
domestic and social duties; and especially
by that intimate union of the creature with

its Creator, which can give merit to our most trifling actions, and which is the means of carrying out the Apostle's admirable advice : 'Whether you eat or drink, or whatsoever else you do, do all to the glory of God.'

The misery of the worldly woman at her last hour will be, that she has lost her time. The hours which God gave her wherewith to gain eternity, and which she has not filled with good works, will rise up against her to condemn her.

But with the Saints, on the contrary, every minute of their lives will be precious in the sight of God, and will merit for them fresh degrees of glory.

O, what an abundant harvest might not our glorious Patriarch St. Joseph expect from all the days, the months, and the years which he devoted entirely to the service and the love of his Saviour!

May his example induce us to begin at once a serious reformation in the employment of that time which so soon will have ceased to exist for us !

EIGHTEENTH DAY.

ON WORK.

' Man is born to labour, and the bird to fly.' JOB.

WHEN God created man, it was not His will that he should be an inactive being. After He had called him out of nothing, He 'took man, and put him into the paradise of pleasure, to dress it and to keep it.'

And this easy occupation would have been to him but a pleasure without any fatigue, for 'work was not yet born into the world.' And the earth would abundantly have repaid his care, and he would have had the satisfaction of producing with his own hands flowers and fruit according to his desires; but our first parents sinned, and it is to their sin that we are always obliged to return, in order to understand the conditions of our present life.

God said to Adam, ' Cursed is the earth

in thy work; with labour and toil shalt thou
eat thereof all the days of thy life.

'Thorns and thistles shall it bring forth
to thee; and thou shalt eat the herbs of the
earth.

'In the sweat of thy face shalt thou eat
bread, till thou return to the earth, out of
which thou wast taken.'

All the generations which were to follow
after Adam and Eve were included in this
curse, so that we may with truth repeat with
Job, 'Man is born to labour as the bird is
to fly.'

And when the Son of God came down
from heaven and became incarnate, He willed
to endure to the full, for the space of thirty
years, the consequences of this condemna-
tion. He deigned to employ Himself as a
carpenter, and gain His bread in the sweat
of His brow. Mary, His mother, led a life
of labour and of privation; and St. Joseph
gives us also the grand example of a descen-
dant of the great King David joyfully sub-
mitting himself to the decree which went
forth against all men without exception. For

this reason it is that St. Paul says, 'He who will not work, neither shall he eat;' and, again, 'Labour as a good soldier of Christ Jesus.'

Work also includes labour, effort; it is a struggle with difficulty. Work is trouble; it is action, but action accompanied with pain; it is pain itself, and therefore is it that in human language the same word is used to express work and pain, *labour;* and work thus defined is the law of life, presenting itself to each individual in a different form.

All the triumphs achieved by men over physical nature, within the last six thousand years, are the result of work; the philosopher, the poet, the artist, each and all struggle and work to attain the end they have in view.

If God has placed us in a social position, which raises us exteriorly above our fellow creatures, we are tempted to look upon ourselves as beings of a different order from the rest of humanity, and to exempt ourselves from the universal sentence. But the Holy Spirit has Himself drawn the picture of 'the

valiant woman;' and it would be well for us
to study in the Holy Scriptures themselves
what are the qualities which ought to belong
to our sex : ' She hath sought wool and flax,
and hath wrought by the counsel of her
hands,' &c.

One of the greatest misfortunes of a great
many women is that they do not know how
to occupy themselves. Their life is passed
in inaction; the least effort, and consequently
the smallest attempt at work, frightens them;
for I do not call work those passing amusements which are but taken up as a pastime.
Like the sluggard, we are afraid to undertake
anything; like him, we dare not; we see a
thousand obstacles in the way, and we forget too much that ' an idle woman is a burden which the earth bears unwillingly.'* Yet
we have a very important mission. Why
then, whilst our fathers and our husbands
are perhaps fulfilling important duties in the
world, do we allow our own lives to assume
that character of vagueness and uncertainty
which imprints itself on all things, even on

* St. John Chrysostom.

good ones, where energy is wanting? Our work, the work which specially belongs to us, is the management of our homes and of our servants; the care of the poor and sick; and the performance of all necessary duties. We should observe that to work is not only to use the spade or the hammer, but diligently to fulfil the mission intrusted to each one of us. When the Holy Spirit praises the 'valiant woman,' that woman whose husband was noble, and who had her servants and her extensive property to look after, He says of her, 'that she hath not eaten her bread in idleness.' (Prov. xxxi. 27.)

'The mind has its labours; study has its weariness. The management of a family, the incessant work which it entails, every position in the world, in fact, has in it something that is laborious and painful; something which, by taxing to the uttermost the body or the mind, causes the general penalty to be shared by each of us individually.' (Mgr. Lecourtier.)

If we looked seriously into our consciences, in order to examine before God what is the work which He requires of us, our duties would stand out clearly before us; and casting aside the futilities which absorb our days, we should soon go through their course with the energy given to us by faith. Surely in these days, when such distress and misery exist on every side, when such multitudes of children are perishing for want of care, and when souls are being lost by thousands— souls for whom Christ died, there can be no lack of work for every one of us according to our capacity. Can we not visit the sick in hospitals or in their own homes, and take them some little delicacy from our own tables? Can we not rescue some little child, wandering and deserted in our big towns? Or should our health incapacitate us from active works like these, cannot our needles clothe the naked, adorn the tabernacles, help the foreign missions?

Cannot our pens be turned to better account than in scribbling useless notes, or filling sheets of paper to some gossiping acquaintance? The want of good books, to counteract the evil literature of the day, is felt on every side. Can we do nothing to supply the need? We are fond of painting. Can we not thus help to adorn some neglected sanctuary? We have taste for music. Can we not assist some village choir by giving them good hymns or chants, or by playing at Benediction in case of need?

I should have wished to have spoken here more extensively of the many and great duties which the law of work imposes on us.

Let me at least remind you that our hands ought continually to be used in the service of our neighbour. To work for the poor is certainly more pleasing in God's sight than to give them our gold: and we may do this in a thousand ways. We have not only hands which we must use, but also minds which we ought not allow to remain fallow. 'I do not wish to make *learned women* of you, in the ridiculous sense given to the word; and yet my desire is that you should not be ignorant of all that raises the mind and ennobles the heart,' writes Mgr. Landriot. He continues:

' A woman's soul is of the same origin as

that of a man; and she too requires to be instructed and enlightened. It is a heavenly plant, which must not be left stunted and barren; it must yield its fruit. And to this end she must labour, so as to be really a helpmeet to her husband.

' A certain amount of knowledge will never hurt a woman; it will help her to put her ideas in order, which is often the only thing wanting in certain minds. Knowledge corrects the judgment, fortifies the will, and gives a certain solidity and dignity to the whole conduct. When, therefore, with your busy hands you have spun the wool and the flax, I should like you to be able to carry on intelligently a conversation on some serious matter, or to meditate on a book of which the chief subject should be something grand or noble.'

Add to all this what Fénélon so well calls the modesty of science in women, and you will deserve that these words should be applied to you : ' A woman of understanding is the friend of silence; nothing is equal to a wise woman.' (Mgr. Landriot.)

NINETEENTH DAY.

ON FILIAL PIETY.

'And He was subject to them.' St. Luke.

In our preceding meditations we have passed
in review our duties towards God. We have
asked ourselves how we could render to Him
that which is due from the creature to his
Creator. It now remains for us to discover
in what manner we are to be just towards
our fellow-creatures.

We must remember that faith ought to
guide us in everything throughout our lives,
and that it is God whom the Christian sees
in his neighbour. This is a fundamental
principle, and we will start from it to-day
in order to examine what are our duties towards our superiors. God has given His
spiritual authority to the Church, and He
has established in society a double hier-
archy—a natural as well as a moral one.

We all of us have superiors, who are to us representatives of divine authority : ' Let every soul be subject to higher powers, for there is no power but from God ; and those that are, are ordained of God,' says the Apostle. It is a question here of superiors in a social and political point of view, and for us women, submission is not in this case difficult.

The first authority to which we have to submit, on the threshold of existence, is that authority at once so great, so loving, and so noble, of our father and mother.

' Hear, O Israel, and observe to do the things which the Lord hath commanded thee.

' Honour thy father and thy mother, that thou mayest live a long time on the earth.

' Honour thy father and thy mother with all thy heart, and forget not the sorrow of thy mother.

' He that feareth the Lord honoureth his parents, and will serve them as his masters that brought him into the world.

' Honour thy father, in work and word,

L

and all patience, that a blessing may come upon thee from him, and his blessing may remain in the latter end.

' He that honoureth his mother is as one that layeth up a treasure. The father's blessing establisheth the houses of the children; but the mother's curse rooteth up the foundation.

' Children, hear the judgment of your father, and so do that you may be saved. For God hath made the father honourable to the children, and seeking the judgment of the mothers hath confirmed it upon the children. Of what an evil fame is he that forsaketh his father; and he is cursed of God that angereth his mother.' (Deut. iv. 1.)

' Fathers and mothers are to their children the direct representatives of God on earth; their tenderness, their care, are, as it were, the images of His divine perfections; and when they understand the sublimity of their office, a reflection of His adorable majesty seems to rest upon them. Therefore it is that amongst all the different kinds of respect and honour which we are called on to

render, none is more sacred than the respect
due to parents. It is the respect of rever-
ence, the respect of affection; and although
it is not the respect of adoration, it is yet a
religious respect.' (Mgr. Dupanloup.) We
must, then, say with the Scriptures : ' Children, obey your parents in the Lord, for
this is just.'

The unfortunate tendency of our own days
is to do away with every mark of deference or
respect towards parents, and we shall have
occasion to remark upon this more than
once, when we study our duty to our neighbour. It is the inevitable consequence of
the want of faith as the mainspring of our
actions.

The divine law establishes a certain distance between superiors and inferiors ; between those who have the right to command,
and those whose duty it is to obey ; and it
is this distance which people wish to ignore,
if not to destroy altogether.

Formerly, the father, the head of the
family, was consulted by his son about everything, and every word of his became a com-

mand. The young man was not, as in these
days, in a very fever of haste to rid himself
of all paternal authority and to enjoy his
liberty. He trembled, certainly, in his father's presence; but his feelings were a
mixture of love and fear. His mother was
the especial object of his affection and respect; what confidence did he not place in
her! what deference was shown to her
slightest wish! Listen to the Count de
Maistre:

'My mother was to me an angel to whom
God had lent a body; my happiness con-
sisted in trying to find out what she wished
me to do; I was like the youngest of my
sisters in her hands.'

But now the young man no longer trembles; his parents' wishes are a burden to
him; family life wearies him; and well is
it if he does not go so far as to deserve the
curse pronounced in the Scriptures:

'The eye that mocketh at his father, and
that despiseth his mother, let the ravens of
the brooks pick it out, and the young eagles
eat it.' (Prov. xxx. 17.)

And if this want of respect, if this craving for liberty, are more evident in our brothers than among ourselves, can we say that we have nothing to reproach ourselves with in this respect? Alas, have we no example of young girls being wanting in deference and submission towards their mothers, neglecting their wishes, and determined to follow their own will in everything? Have we not even seen some who, when raised to a social position, which they owe to the sacrifices made by their parents, have actually ended by despising them and being ashamed of them?

Let us, then, be grateful and full of tenderness towards those to whom we owe our existence, our education, and all that we are. Let us not complain of the yoke which, no doubt, other duties will make us some day regret. O, sweet and easy are a child's duties! It is sweet to be the joy and the consolation of those we love: it is easy to obey the orders of a father and of a mother who only desire our happiness!

The life of our Divine Master, who, together with His laws, has set us such a perfect example, ought to be a powerful encouragement to us to practise this great virtue. Of the thirty-three years which He passed on the earth, thirty of them were spent in the practice of obedience, and are summed up in the Gospels in these words: 'He was subject to them.'

Jesus obeying the commands of Joseph and Mary—here is our model. With how much respect, with how much tender care, did He not surround them! And when, later on, He returned to His kingdom, what a glorious throne did He not prepare for her! He makes her Queen of Angels, Queen of Saints, and grants her that power of intercession which was to make her the Help of Christians, and the Refuge of sinners.

And in these later days are we not told how, even in heaven, Jesus listens with a sort of filial submission to the repeated supplications addressed to Him by our holy Patriarch, as well as by His Mother?

TWENTIETH DAY.

FAMILY LIFE.

' Let the women learn in silence with all subjection.'
St. Paul.

WHEN God called forth the world out of chaos, He spoke but one word; but when He was about to create man, He paused. ' Let Us make man to Our image and likeness.' After that He says, ' It is not good for man to be alone;' so that it is out of goodness and love that He created woman. ' Let Us make him a help like unto himself, that he might have a comfort and support during his sojourn on earth.

' This implied much; for although the natural superiority and primacy of man is strongly recognised, it shows that he is neither so great nor so self-sufficing as not to stand in need of support, comfort, and sympathy; it thus established the authority of him who in the order of nature was to command and to direct, whilst at the same time it secured him from the temptation of pride.'

Mgr. Dupanloup adds:

'It established the dignity of the woman, who was to counsel and support him, whilst at the same time it saved her from the dangers inherent in her natural weakness, and even if we may say so, from the possible temptations of vanity.'

'It would be impossible,' exclaims Tertullian, 'to find words which can express all the excellence of Christian marriage. The Church ties the knot, the offering of the Holy Sacrifice confirms it, the blessing of the priest puts the seal to it, angels witness it, and our Heavenly Father ratifies it; and how holy is the union of two Christians, thus bound together by the same hopes, by the same vows, by the same rule of life, living both in the same state of dependence on God; it may in truth be said that they are but one flesh, and animated by but one soul.

'They pray together, they perform their religious and penitential exercises together;

their whole life is an example, a very model of charity and holiness; you see them together at church and at the Table of the Lord; everything is shared in common—cares, troubles, joys, and pleasures. There are no secrets between them, nothing but perfect confidence and love. They need not conceal their good deeds from each other; but together they go about visiting the sick, helping the poor, distributing their charities, sacrificing themselves, and attending zealously to every duty, without either reserve or constraint. At their frugal repasts they may make the sign of the cross and say their grace openly, without fear of ridicule; and together they raise their voices to Almighty God in hymns of thanksgiving and praise.

'Their only rivalry is that of vying with each other in fervour in the service of God. Such marriages rejoice the Heart of Jesus Christ, and He blesses them and gives them His peace.' (Tertullian.)

Can we find a more perfect picture of a real Christian union than this? Centuries

have gone by since it was written; but surely
we ourselves have seen, here and there, examples of such marriages; lives so full of
holiness and goodness, that one is tempted
to look upon them as the realisation of one's
dreams rather than reality.

Alas, side by side with these happy
unions, how many others come before one
in which the basis of all real happiness, the
sharing of the same faith and the same hope,
is entirely wanting !

Whether these unhappy marriages are
the result of worldly ambition on the part
of the parents, or of excessive imprudence
in young girls, the consequences are equally
disastrous. 'And in such cases, the mono-
tony of each succeeding day, and the chain of
the ever-recurring duties and cares which
marriage entails, become wearisome and
even irritating, where they are not accepted
in a spirit of generosity and devotedness ;
for if, in their mutual lives, married people
do not obey the great law of Christianity
—the law of self-denial and self-control—
if, on the contrary, they give free vent to

every impulse, following the momentary
inclinations of their tempers and dispositions,
and resenting little mortifications and vexations, then neither order nor harmony is
possible. They have begun to slide down an
inclined plane where there is no stopping ;
every morning the troubles and disputes
of the preceding day are taken up afresh,
and the irritation and ill-feeling, which are
perhaps the result of whole years of mis-
understanding, thus daily become worse and
worse.

' It seems impossible to forgive and to forget, and patiently to make a fresh start,
with renewed courage and trust; and one
would imagine that there must exist some
hidden source of bitterness and of enmity
for ever troubling lives which ought to
have been happy and peaceful.' (Père de
Ravignan.)

A woman's first duty is obedience; and
let us here observe, that this obedience is
all the more difficult for the very reason of
the intimate relations that exist between
husband and wife. It is easier to obey a

father than a husband. The former has the authority of age; our affection for him is full of respect and deference, and it seems natural that he should command; but a husband is on an equality with us; he is of our generation. In a general way he leaves us more freedom than did our parents, so that when he does exercise his authority it seems hard to us, and we are disposed to rebel.

Did we not hope to have more liberty when we were married? and now we already feel the chain.

And yet, after all, have we the right to complain?

If we read the history of our own sex before Christianity, we shall find that nothing can equal the almost universal despotism and degradation which, during the course of forty centuries, one-half of mankind imposed upon the other.

The Gospel has saved us from such hard slavery, and nothing is now required of us but what would seem right in the natural order of creation. Let us never forget that man is the head of the family, and as such is entitled to respect and obedience.

The most perfect creature who ever came out of the hands of God is, of course, the Blessed Virgin. In the order of grace, and in consideration of the high dignity which our Lord bestowed upon her, it is evident that she was placed above St. Joseph; and yet what happened at Bethlehem and at Nazareth? God still preserved the order which He had Himself established; it is the head of the family to whom He addresses Himself; it is to him that the angel speaks when he is the bearer of God's commands; above all, it is St. Joseph whom Mary obeys without a murmur.

In order to give us a true notion of the obedience which is due from a woman to her husband, the Apostle expresses the command in the most formal manner. But what is to be the degree and the nature of our obedience? Listen: ' Christian women, be submissive and obedient unto your husbands, *as unto Jesus Christ.*'

Much is contained in these last words.

There is but one principle of authority. In the absolute sense of the words, it is God alone who can say to His creature, 'Thou shalt obey Me.' Our superiors have a right over us, in virtue of the delegated power given them by God, and it is this which ought to render obedience easy to us; it is this also which places limits to this very authority; for, from the moment that the will of our superiors is in contradiction to the will of God when distinctly expressed, it becomes our duty to obey God rather than man.

To render obedience to a father, to a mother, to a husband—to a master, if one is a servant; to a superior, if one is a religious—is in fact to render obedience to God. Thus will obedience be supernaturalised, and become one of the highest Christian virtues.

Let us not, however, wonder, if we find difficulties in the practice of obedience. Sin has left a seed of rebellion at the bottom of our hearts, which we shall find it hard to conquer. We shall have to fight, and fight valiantly, before we can bring ourselves to submit; but it is especially of the obedience of women to their husbands that the Bible refers in the words : ' Let women be subject to their husbands, as to the Lord.' (Ephesians v. 22.)

How often may not some sacrifice of our own will, cheerfully and joyfully made, appease anger and irritation, and be the means of forming a yet closer bond between those whom God has united by the Holy Sacrament of Marriage ; whilst, on the contrary, obstinacy and tenacity of our own will may easily tear asunder two souls whom God had created for each other.

We have all of us, alas, a thirst for independence which we do not attempt to control. Let us accustom ourselves to look upon our husband as a master. If he be kind, gentle, and indulgent, then obedience will be easy, and we may thank God for it. If he be hard, unjust, overbearing, still must we submit; and should God require that we should give up our own tastes and pleasures for the sake of pleasing our husbands, we may rest assured that He will not fail to give us grace and courage, that we may crush our own wishes and desires, and offer them up as a willing sacrifice to Him.

However happy a marriage may be, trials and troubles will come sooner or later. To all of us the work of salvation must be a work of self-denial. Hence it is that a writer, distinguished as much for her piety as for her learning, compares a Christian woman to the nun in her convent. 'Women do not sufficiently consider,' she says, 'that when they marry, they too make a vow of poverty; for do they not give over their fortune into the hands of their husband, and are only able to dispose of it according to his pleasure?

'They make also a vow of obedience to their husbands, and even one of chastity, inasmuch as it is no longer lawful to them to try and please any other man.' (Mdme. de Lamartine.)

Marriage considered in this light will no longer be the cruel disappointment it too often has been; neither will so many bitter tears be shed by young women, who have not understood the holiness of Christian marriage, or the duties it entails.

TWENTY-FIRST DAY.

FAMILY LIFE (*continued*).

'The unbelieving husband is sanctified by the wife.' ST. PAUL.

OBEDIENCE is not a woman's only duty towards her husband; and, as we said yesterday, the Holy Spirit has Himself in the Scriptures defined her mission. It is her part, also, to help and support him whom she has chosen for her lord and master.

Faith alone can explain what first strikes us as an enigma: man is strong and vigorous, woman weak and delicate; he is the master, she is not, it is true, his slave, but his submissive helpmate; and yet the Bible speaks truly when it tells us that she ought also to be man's consolation and support. We have already seen that life must be looked upon as a time of trial, full of labour, pain, weariness, and agony of heart. Listen to the words

of a holy bishop addressing himself to women :
' You are born to suffer, because you possess
far more than man the capability of suffering ; with few exceptions, he knows not how
to suffer ; he cannot bear pain; and whenever
there comes upon him any evil, however
slight, however evanescent, it is too much for
him, and he requires woman to help and comfort him.' (Mgr. Mermillod.)

'Since the fall of man, there is nothing here
below which commands such universal respect, almost, we may say, homage, nothing
which is in itself so great or so dignified, as
the calm and patient endurance of a great
sorrow. Well, I must confess it, men are
seldom capable of such endurance. Not so
with women. When a family is struck down
by some terrible affliction—the loss of a dear-
ly loved son, or of a cherished daughter—
how often do we not see the man—the father
—break down, crushed to the earth ; the woman—the mother—she, too, is crushed, yet
she bears up. You see that she was born to
suffer ; that she understands to the full the
act of suffering ; and that, according to the

beautiful words of Holy Scripture, she has learnt all the secrets both of sorrow and of infirmity. There is something in her which is ever steadfast and immovable, something strong and invincible in the midst of the very ruins of her own heart.' (Mgr. Dupanloup.)

Besides the great sorrows of life, there are the troubles and the worries of our every-day existence. In the busy life of the world, in which men, in the exercise of their different callings, are obliged to mix, vexations, and misunderstandings, and annoyances, are things of daily occurrence; and who can chase away and soothe vexation of spirit— who can cheer the downcast heart, infusing into it fresh hope and fresh courage—who, indeed, but woman, with that exquisite tact and delicacy which God has bestowed upon her?

The life of the Holy Family at Nazareth is well calculated to teach us this truth. If it is St. Joseph who is its protector and its support, it is the Blessed Virgin who is, as it were, the angel-comforter in every trial; and she makes use of the intimate union in which she is privileged to live with Almighty God, to help him whom she has accepted as her spouse to advance daily in the paths of perfection ; thus setting an example to all Christian women of the greatest of their duties, *i.e.* to lead upwards, towards life eternal, those to whom they have been united on earth ; for 'this temporal union is but an image of the yet sweeter union, which will have neither time nor end, in the bosom of God.' (Mgr. Dupanloup.)

'To aid man to work out his salvation ought to be woman's chief object; her mission, her ministry, her glory, her grandeur, and her dignity. Thus it is that woman receives from God a sort of religious authority, we might almost say a religious consecration. She is, in one sense, the *priest* of the family, just as man is the king.' (Le P. Ventura.)

Our sex is called the pious sex ; and if we look through the history of the Church we shall see what a foremost place Christian women, both as wives and mothers, have always occupied in the merciful designs of

Providence; we need only instance St. Monica, St. Paula, St. Clotilde, Blanche of Castille, St. Elizabeth of Hungary; and here, surely, are examples enough to animate our zeal and courage.

'I conjure you more than ever to let these great Christian truths take possession of your minds; do not rest content with the conventional teaching learnt in your childhood, but endeavour to raise your minds to the regions of truth and reality, and try to understand the intellectual duties which are binding on you. Faith can no longer be a sort of family heritage; it is a treasure which must be preserved and developed.'

'Strive also to be amongst those who know how to forget and sacrifice themselves for others; be full of faith and of the spirit of self-devotion. Like the martyrs of old, so ought woman to conquer, by resignation, by patience, by courage, and by faith; and let us never doubt that *everything is possible to her who believes.*' (Mdme. de Marcey.)

Your honestly expressed convictions will arrest incipient doubt, and stay the march of

incredulity; whilst the sight of your holy devotedness to the good of others will put a
barrier to the monstrous increase of selfishness which is ever threatening to freeze up
our hearts and embitter the peace of our
homes.

Especially when a woman has the, alas,
but too common misfortune to find herself
united to a man without principles and without faith, she must never cease repeating to
herself that not one of her actions is indifferent in its results. In the eyes of her husband she is the impersonification of religion;
the faults she commits are, in his sight, the
faults of her faith; just as, on the other hand,
he knows, though he will not own it, that all
the good that is in her is produced by religion. If she be good and gentle, it is her
faith which makes her so; if she be cross
and dissatisfied, it is religion which is in
fault; if she be submissive and devoted, he
blesses in his heart the faith which bears
such fruits; if she be rebellious and capri-
cious, religion appears to him as a monster
and a bugbear.

There is a language understood by all, there are words intelligible to all, which can be used, especially by women, with a double advantage both to themselves and others; I mean the language of holiness, the preaching by example, the strong though silent influence of gentleness and self-denial, the convincing and powerful argument of a consistent and constant performance of duty. ' The chief proof of our virtue,' says Montaigne, ' is our virtue.' ' It is by persuasion and by gentleness that we must seek to save souls.' (St. Gregory of Nazianzen.)

And when we have reached that elevation of mind which is the real atmosphere of a Christian woman, desires of self-gratification, of self-love, of vanity, as well as of the enjoyment of the fleeting pleasures of this world, will come to us only like distant echoes, which we hardly hear, and which will leave us undisturbed.

What, indeed, in comparison with the glorious realities of our faith, are all those miserable worldly interests, in which so many, who call themselves Christian women, are entirely engrossed? What sorrow and remorse are they not laying up for themselves! and what bitter tears will they not one day shed, when, too late, they discover their mistake! But, on the other hand, what consolation, what pure and unalloyed joy, is in store for that woman, who after years, it may be, of sacrifice and of suffering, shall at last succeed in bringing back to God the husband who had strayed far from Him!

O how, in that blessed day, will all sorrow be forgotten, and the overflowing heart only burst forth into songs of thanksgiving and joy! And if the last hours of him, who owes to her his salvation, are hours of God's mercy and pardon to his soul, her happiness will be indeed a supernatural one; for ' if we believe in heaven for those we love, can we lament that those whom we cherish should be happy a little sooner than ourselves?' (Madame Albert de la Ferronnays.)

TWENTY-SECOND DAY.

ON THE EDUCATION OF CHILDREN.

'Feed the flock which God has committed to you.'
ST. PAUL.

CHRISTIAN marriage is, under the Gospel law, the foundation of society. It is the sacred institution of the family.

'It is not only for the sake of giving birth to children that Almighty God permits fathers and mothers to participate in His power, wisdom, and love. It is that they may bring up aright those little lives which have been intrusted to them; so that their children's characters may be formed in accordance with the laws of God, and that all those noble faculties may be developed in them which constitute the dignity of human nature.

' We must, then, lay down the broad prin-

ciple, that the first duty of parents is to
bring up the children whom God has given
them in accordance with His laws.' (Mgr.
Dupanloup.)

It is impossible to treat so vast and important a subject in a few lines. Many
admirable books have been written on this
grave matter. We hardly dare touch upon
it farther than by a few words, which may
serve as an invitation to more serious reading on the subject.

The father and mother are here below the
depositors of divine authority. ' God creates
men, but it is on their education that their
whole future depends. This work is the
highest which can be undertaken, for it is
the continuation of the divine operation in
its most important part.' (Mgr. Dupanloup.)

' A whole generation passes through a certain system of education, and comes out of
it like a statue, the composition for which
has been run in a mould.' (L'Abbé de Cleure.)

We may then exclaim with Liebnitz, 'that
to give to youth a good and sound education
is really laying the foundation of all human

happiness. And that we should reform the world if we could only reform its education.'

'Like the Church,' writes Mgr. Gaume, 'the family has been established to watch over the spiritual life of the new-born child. It is by the fireside, on his mother's knee, in his father's arms, that this little child, who is the heir of eternity, must receive the first knowledge of his noble origin, of his grave duties, and of his sublime destiny. The youthful candidate for heaven must there learn that to be one of the elect, he must live for God and for his brethren. It is there, in a word, that he must make his glorious apprenticeship in all Christian virtues, which is the only road to eternal happiness.'

'Remember, above everything, that nothing is small or to be lightly regarded, where the consequences are so serious; that nothing must be neglected, where the results of such negligence, increasing with the age of the victim, attain to such fearful proportions when the child is grown to man's estate. And remembering those words which have so often been verified, " man is, all his life,

what he was on his mother's knee," strive
to make him pious, obedient, and submissive
then, so that he may be one day virtuous,
wise, and good. It would be better to die
without children, than to leave behind one
an ungodly and irreligious seed.' (Mdme. de
Marcey.)

Education, having for its main object that
of bringing up children—by which we mean
training them—is a slow, gradual, and pro-
gressive work; and, according to the famous
saying of Fénélon, it should follow and help
the individual nature of each; and be carried
on, as St. François de Sales so admirably
expresses it, bit by bit, little by little, with
much pains and infinite patience.

The mother is the natural teacher, given
to her children by God Himself. On her
the first stage of their education entirely
rests. The father, absorbed in occupations
which necessarily involve his being away
from home during the greater part of the
day, only sees his child from time to time
during the first years of this important work.

The love of a mother for her child is so

deeply ingrained in her heart, that God did not think it necessary to make it the object of a special commandment. When He wishes to paint the infinity of His love for us, He can find no better comparison than this : ' Can a woman forget her infant, so as not to have pity on the son of her womb ? Yea, she may forget ; yet will not I forget thee.'

After all, it must be allowed that we are more ready to love our children too much than too little. We often make little idols of them ; we love them amiss ; for their own sakes, because we spoil them ; for ours, because we have too strong and *human* an affection for them. And this brings us back to that great principle in the life of a Christian which teaches us to supernaturalise our affections.

When a mother takes her new-born child in her arms, she asks herself this question, while fixing on him a scrutinising look : ' What future is reserved for him ? What will he be ?' And, losing herself in a dream, she builds up a whole scaffolding of ambi-

tious projects for this cherished being. What
will he be? Alas, who can tell? Will the
course of his life run smoothly and happily?
or will he be exposed to every kind of suffering and trial in its course? Will our
Lord give him health and length of days?
or will He cut short the thread? We can
only read the history of the past; the future
is hidden from us. But that which we
cannot doubt is, that under this fragile and
delicate earthly form a heart beats and a
soul exists; a soul called to the noblest
destinies hereafter; a heart created to love
God. Above all, we know that this child
will be, in a religious point of view, whatever his mother makes him.

Fénélon expresses this thought with a
marvellous lucidity. 'The brain of a little
child is soft, hot, and damp, which causes
him to be continually in motion. This soft-
ness of brain enables everything to be easily
impressed upon it, and all visible objects
leave an indelible mark; thus we should
hasten to write on these little heads while
the characters are easily formed. But one

must choose with care the pictures we wish engraved on them; for in so small and precious a receptacle we should only pour choice things. Let us always recollect that at this age we should only fill the mind with that which we wish should remain there through life. The first impressions, given while the brain is soft, and as yet like a sheet of white paper, are the deepest. They harden in proportion as age dries it up; and then they become ineffaceable.'

The duty of a mother to watch over this, the earliest stage of her child's education, is such that nothing can dispense her from it. It must be our care to develop the germ of all good and noble qualities in their little minds; to watch the first awakening of their intelligence; to join their little hands in prayer, and to teach them to lisp two of the sweetest words which the human tongue can pronounce — 'Jesus' and 'Mary.'

If we had lived in the days when our Saviour traversed the plains of Judea, how happy we should have been to hear those words from His lips: 'Suffer the little children to come unto Me, for of such is the kingdom of heaven.'

Well, to-day our mission is the same: to lead to the feet of our Divine Master those little beings whose pure souls He has given us in trust. Have we ever thought of how sacred a thing a little child is, fresh from the waters of baptism, and whose innocent robe is as yet unstained with a single sin? The father of Origen used to uncover the breast of his boy and say, 'I adore the Holy Spirit, who has deigned to take up His abode in the heart of my child.' With what tender respect and solicitude should we not surround this little being, who can only be compared to one of God's holy angels in heaven!

Let us learn from St. Joseph the respect which is due to holy infancy. See him take the Infant Jesus in his arms. Ah, it was not only the temple of the living God which he venerated, when Jesus covered him with tender kisses; it was God Himself. Let us place under his tutelar care, and under that of Mary, that queen of mothers, the efforts which we may make to preserve intact in our children's souls that purity which makes them brothers of Jesus Christ and heirs of heaven.

And let us often repeat, kneeling by the cradle which holds the object of our fondest hopes, those admirable words of Blanche of Castille, 'My son, God only knows how I love you! But I would rather see you deprived of your kingdom, and even of your life, than soiled by one mortal sin.'

TWENTY-THIRD DAY.

EDUCATION OF CHILDREN (*continued*).

'The words of parents are as eloquent books to their children.' ST. CHRYSOSTOM.

THE Christian mother has in her hands three great powers, of which she ought alternately to make use for the education of her children: prayer, authority, and example.

In prayer certainly lies our greatest strength, and did we but know how to use it, the results we should obtain would be wonderful. O, if but each of our children could say of their mother what St. Gregory of Nazianzen used to relate of his: 'Prayer was each day her best and principal nourishment.' Let us recall to mind with what fervour our supplications rose up to heaven, on that day when death seemed hovering over the cradle of our be-

loved child. It was then that it might well be
said, that each of our groans was a prayer.
But, alas, if the danger has mercifully
passed away from the one so dear to us,
are there not other dangers which are constantly threatening the soul which has been
confided to our care? Are we not in continual want of God's help to fulfil our noble
mission towards him?

Let us then pray, and never cease pray-
ing. And to prayer, let us join action; for
God has placed our children in our hands,
and, as St. Jerome tells us: 'He has made
us their guide, their master, and their judge.

'Have I not given thee all power over
him? In his earliest youth I confided him
to thee, to mould and to direct him ; therefore if thou neglected to correct and restrain
him, what grace hast thou the right to
expect from Me?'

And here we are placed between two
great difficulties: too great indulgence, and
a systematic and rigid severity.

There is a species of indulgence which is
only weakness; let us be kind, but firm.

Alas, this child, whom we shrink from reproving and correcting, because we will not make him shed a few tears, which would soon be dried again, how soon will he not be obliged to bend his will to that of his fellow-creatures, even to the force of circumstances ? If you have a son, ' bow down his neck while he is young, and beat him while he is a child, lest he grow stubborn, and regard thee not, and so be a sorrow of heart to thee.' (Ecclus. xxx. 12.)

And our daughters, are they not destined to bear later on the yoke of marriage, to submit their will to that of their husbands ?

Our severity must not, however, have in it anything unjust or exaggerated. An authority which is really sure of its own power is patient and inflexible, maintaining itself without anger, and enforcing its commands without violence. But to arrive at this result, we must take care that our orders shall not be too multiplied. There are parents who make the great mistake of assuming continually with their children a tone of command, even about the most trifling things. They order and forbid, when they hardly need have expressed a wish, or offered a word of advice; they abuse their authority, in fact, and God only knows to what such abuse may lead.

When a serious thing is in question, issue your commands with gentleness and firmness. Never let a child gain by its tears and entreaties what you have thought fit to refuse a few moments before; for that would be weakness, and you would teach him that the best means to get his own way is by importunity. But when it cannot injure either his health or his character, that he should do one thing instead of another, and choose for himself his lesson or his play, O, then, leave the poor child the innocent use of his liberty!

Neither should you allow a child to feel the influence of your own momentary humour and dispositions; to-day, perhaps, we feel happy and cheerful, and our child's fun amuses us; to-morrow, we may be sad or melancholy; but why should the poor child, who is not aware of any change in us, and

who besides could not understand it even if
he did, be expected to be less merry than
the day before? We must also be very
careful not to give him false notions, by in-
flicting on him punishments which are not
in proportion to the gravity of his fault.
If, for instance, a child is careless or clumsy,
if he breaks by mistake something of value,
then let us be patient and indulgent; when
a thing vexes and annoys us, we generally
think too much of the consequences of it,
and of the harm it does to us, without sufficiently considering the intention of the person who did it. But a disregard of truth
or of justice, a disrespectful answer, a fit of
passion, obstinacy, or idleness—faults such
as these must be punished, and severely
punished.

Let us not spoil our children; let us take
every necessary care of their health, but
without all that enervating delicacy which
is rather injurious than salutary; just as
their food should be wholesome but simple,
and their clothes suitable but not luxurious.

'If you wish to secure to your child a

happy future, treat his body as if he were
the son of a peasant, and his soul as if he
were the son of a king; give him the physical powers of a plebeian, and the mental
qualities of a gentleman; so that his tastes
and wishes being as simple as those of the
former, his generosity and liberality may
equal the latter.'

'Learn to distinguish always clearly in
him what a very clever man has called the
"animal and the angel," which is the same
as that which St. Paul speaks of as "the
old man and the new," or the terrestrial man
and the celestial. Deal roughly with the
animal, but respect the angel.'

'Let us often visit in spirit that humble
home at Nazareth, where Jesus dwells, that
model Son; and Mary and Joseph, those
model parents. Let us imitate their spirit
of simplicity and austerity of life; nothing
useless, no luxury, and yet what hidden
riches!'

'Let us, also, endeavour to make our
children rich; not, indeed, in gold, or silver,
or lands, but rich in piety, in wisdom, and

in virtue; thus will they have fewer wants,
and the goods of this world will not be held
by them in such high estimation.'

' A mother's third great power of influence
is the influence of example.' (St. John Chrysostom.)

' Let your children one day have in remembrance more what they have seen you
do than what you have said to them.' (Curé
d'Ars.)

' How can you dare to recommend to your
children gentleness and patience, if you give
way before them to temper and passion ?
How can you inculcate truth, if you tell
falsehoods ; or simplicity, whilst you make
such a show of luxury ; or the love of useful
work, when you are given up to pleasure;
or modesty, if your dress offends against it ;
or charity, if you turn away from the poor
who implore your aid ?' (St. Jerome.)

' If a child sees its mother, who is its
example and its oracle, give up without
hesitation all the advantages which may be
purchased by a certain degree of unscrupu-
lousness ; brave without false shame, in the

face of a positive duty, every kind of human respect, and boldly confront the blame and the censures of the world; if, in fact, she shows by her whole life that she will ever obey God rather than man, in how great esteem will he not hold the duty of obedience both to her and to God! What a powerful impression will not her example make upon him! and how valuable will be the strength of mind which he will acquire to enable him, in after life, to resist the force of other examples and other counsels!' (Mdme. de Marcey.)

TWENTY-FOURTH DAY.

EDUCATION OF CHILDREN (*continued*).

'Keep the good thing committed to thy trust by the Holy Ghost, who dwelleth in thee.' St. Paul.

A mother's duty is not over when her child is obliged to leave her, in order that he may receive an education which she could not have given him. It is for her, as well as for the father, to make choice of those to whom they are about to confide all that is dearest and most precious to them in the world. And what judgment and care are not necessary to prevent such a step from being a fatal one to the child's soul? Of course, it is essential that his studies should be such as may fit him to fill an honourable position in the world; but, besides this, and O, far before it! it is essential that the good seed, which has been sown in his heart in his own home, should not be smothered by pernicious and

erroneous teaching. The all important thing
is, that he should grow up a good Christian;
that whilst his mind is developed, the faith
which has been implanted in him should be
preserved intact.

The true mother ought not to abandon her
son in the new life upon which he has en-
tered; she should often see him, write to
him, take an interest in all his pursuits,
and be the confidante of his schoolboy triumphs and defeats, just as she used to be
of his childish joys and sorrows; for soon
will begin for this boy a decisive and dangerous epoch; that time of youth, so fatal
to many, during which his mother's influence will perhaps be the only one which
will in any degree counteract other and pernicious counsels.

' But it is the remembrance of his mother
which is ever recurring to him, and which at
last gains the victory. Often is it the only
thing which, apparently buried and forgotten at the bottom of his heart, has yet the
power of touching or arresting him; and so,
when sorrow or trouble comes upon him, he

instinctively has recourse to her, as, after God, the most natural and safe refuge given to human nature.' (Nicolas.)

We say, then, with the Count de Maistre : ' When once a mother has traced on her son's forehead the impress of divinity, it is almost a certainty that the finger of vice will never efface it.'

' Let us then be steadfast and unmovable, abounding in the work of the Lord, knowing that your labour is not in vain in the Lord.' (St. Paul.)

It is easier to feel than to define that tact inherent in a mother, which, like the experienced eye of a doctor, instinctively teaches when is the right moment to speak and when to be silent; when it is best to act, and when to refrain from interfering; that tact, which in its inexhaustible resources knows always how to suggest a bright idea, soothe a ruffled spirit, and console by a winning smile.

Nothing can replace this wonderful intuition : neither science, nor talent, nor genius. It is a gift which seems to develop itself,

and is innate in those maternal hearts who
understand their mission, and have a real
appreciation of their duty.

' The dwelling-place of this most excellent
gift is in the innermost recesses of the heart,
but its action is almost imperceptible, for it
manifests itself far more by silence than by
words. It sees everything without looking;
it divines thoughts and feelings; it replies
without having been questioned; it has in-
ventions and resources for every emergency;
and it is ever on the watch to ward off
troubles and vexations. Patience and prudence are its constant companions, and its
chief art consists in awaiting the favourable
moment; for its victories are less the effect
of skilful management than of opportune-
ness in choosing the right time for its operations.' (Le P. Ratisbonne.)

Such is the devotion of a mother, ever
varying in its form and expression. Such
mothers understand how necessary it is that
their son's homes should be made pleasant
to them, so that they may not have to seek
elsewhere their excitements and pleasures.

It is a mother's imperative duty to allow their sons to go into society, perhaps the most worldly, and even to encourage it, so as by this means to preserve them from dangerous and bad company.

Well may many a mother, whose misdirected and wrongly conceived piety has caused her to fail in this respect, shed tears of blood over her mistake, for-it may be the very soul of her son which she has risked. O, *that* is not to love the world, to go into it for the sake of one's children; on the contrary, it is to sacrifice oneself; and sacrifice is a magic talisman which takes away from the world its bitterness and danger.

As long as love for his own home and his own family have their place in a young man's heart; as long as the paternal roof has any charm for him, and its pleasures are not despised, so long is there but little to fear for him. He may, it is true, be carried away by bad example, and may for a time neglect his religion, give up the practice of it, and allow his faith to grow cold; but if he keeps his affection for his family; if he can always take pleasure in its quiet joys, and in the innocent amusements of domestic life, he will not be long before he returns to his religious duties. By remaining faithful to his father and mother he will be faithful also to his God; and retaining virtuous habits, he will never become thoroughly irreligious.' (Madame de Marcey.)

Listen to a great orator, who well understood the happiness of family life: ' O home of our fathers, domestic hearth of all Christian nations, home of our childhood, where from our very earliest years we imbibed, as it were, with the very light, the love of holy things, as our years pass on, still do we look back on thee with hearts ever young; and did not eternity beckon us away from thee, we should be inconsolable at seeing thy shadows daily lengthening and thy light fading.' (Le P. Lacordaire.)

It is at this period of her son's life that a mother finds all her strength in prayer. Armed with this weapon, her heart follows her child wherever he may be. Already is he fighting in the plain; let her then, like Moses, remain on the mountain, her hands raised to heaven.   Thus will she imitate St. Monica, who, ' seeing that all her efforts were in vain, and that her son no longer listened to anything, turned herself resolutely to God ; and one day, when the danger was the most imminent, like the unhappy Agar, she sent forth from her very soul such a cry of anguish, such groans of misery and of despair, that God could no longer resist (as He never will resist prayers such as hers) ; and then to her also He gave back her child.   She died of her happiness, leaving as a legacy to all mothers, who, like her, are mourning for their sons, the secret of her own consolation.' (L'Abbé Bougaud.)

TWENTY-FIFTH DAY.

DUTIES TO OUR SERVANTS.

'But if any man have not care of his own, and especially of those of his house, he hath denied the faith, and is worse than an infidel.' TIMOTHY v. 8.

UNDER the pagan dispensation, slavery was an established law. Masters had an absolute right of life and death over their slaves; and we read in history on this subject some fearful traits of cruelty.

The Messiah came upon earth to introduce a new law; and when, Gospel in hand, we study the new relations then established between masters and servants, we find a totally different view of the matter, and one which would have seemed incomprehensible to the pagans. Jesus declares that He came not into the world ' to be ministered unto,

but to minister;' and he who is His Vicar
upon earth, styles himself *the Servant of
servants.*

We are all equal before God, and descended from one common stock. Our souls,
bought with no less a price than the Precious
Blood of Jesus Christ, have the same im-
mortal destiny. Children of God, and joint
heirs of Christ, we all aspire to the glories
of heaven.

'My name is Christian,' was the answer
of one of the most illustrious martyrs of
the Church to his judges. Before God we
have no other distinctive character. Nobility, titles, honours, riches, all disappear
and fall before the Sovereign Master of heaven and earth ; and the same veneration is
felt for the humble shepherdess St. Gene-
vieve or St. Germaine, as towards the great
queens St. Helena or St. Clotilde.

The different ranks of the social hier-
archy are only accidents in human nature;
the point of departure and the ultimate end
are the same for all. These are truths
from which we must draw practical con-

sequences; truths which should be our
guides in our communications with those
whose services have been only lent to us
by God.

It is thus that we shall arrive at being
really just towards them, by giving them
what is their due.

What, then, are our servants? and what
place should they occupy in our households?
Do not let us begin by keeping them at
arm's length, when we consider that their
patron and model is our holy Patriarch
himself.

Do we read in the Gospels that he had
many servants? No. This son of the
kings of Judah esteemed himself happy and
proud to render such services as were in
his power to Jesus and Mary.

Christianity has already assigned to the
servant his rank and place in the family.
He is an adopted child of the house, and is
entitled to a share in the same care and
affection which we bestow on our own off-
spring.

' Our servants are our neighbours and

humble brothers and sisters, whom charity
commands us to love like ourselves. Let
us love them, then; these men and women
who live under our own roof, and eat the
same bread. Let us treat them as we should
like to be treated ourselves, if we were in
their place and in their position.' (St.
Francis of Sales.)

As masters and mistresses, therefore, we
have to fulfil a paternal or maternal func-
tion towards them; in the same way that,
as servants, they are bound to honour in us
an authority of which the source is from
God.

This defines the real relations between
masters and servants; and if they were
thoroughly understood, they would protect
their mutual interests far more than all the
regulations of the penal code. Religion has
not suppressed the distinction between master and servant; but it has sanctified both
one and the other, by showing them in what
way the position of each should be defined.

We ought to take the greatest care in
the choice of our servants, and inquire

carefully as to their antecedents, their principles, and their morality. Our house is like a little kingdom, and we ought not to introduce into it any one capable of disturbing its peace. It is also very essential that the mistress of the house, taking example by the 'valiant woman' in Holy Writ, should trace out exactly the work of each of her servants. Leave as little as possible uncertain and undefined. Whatever may be a woman's position in the world, she may surely give a few minutes every morning to that supervision of her house which only a mistress's eye can supply. Let her orders for the day be clear and explicit, yet given with thorough consideration for the comfort of those under her, and then let her exact a punctual obedience to those commands, so that her rule may be at once kind, just, and firm.

Let us have great gentleness and patience with our servants. They all have faults; but have we not also ours? 'Do not let us, either, undervalue the services they render us,' writes St. Francis of Sales. ' It is expedient to encourage them, by showing them that you are pleased and satisfied with their performance of their duties, and have confidence in them. Let them see that you look upon them as brothers and friends, in whose concerns you have a real interest. In the same way as a puff of wind in the sail sends on the vessel a hundred times faster than the most indefatigable rowing, so a kind and loving word, a mark of interest in their families or themselves, insures exact and even devoted service in your servant, far more than half a dozen harsh and menacing orders.'

Let them feel confident that they may rely on us for wise counsel and kind help in time of need. Above all, do not let us forget that we owe them a good example. O, how much some women will have to answer for in this respect! In exchange for their services, we ought to render them even greater ones, in the spiritual sense. They have given up everything to come to us—liberty, country, family. Our home has become theirs; and we are ourselves as their

visible providence. But we are responsible
before God for their souls; and this should
give us matter of serious reflection.

Let their acquaintances, their goings out
and comings in, be a matter of careful supervision, especially should they be young and
inexperienced. Above all, take care that
they always have the opportunity of attending to their religious duties on Sundays and
Days of Obligation. Lend them good and
amusing books to fill up their idle hours.
We owe them the bread of the soul, as
much as that of the body. Ah, why cannot we follow the good advice which the
Père Lacordaire gave to a young master
of a household? 'Do not forget that a
faithful and affectionate servant is one of
the greatest blessings God can give us, and
an important element in our happiness.
But you will only obtain such, by caring
for his soul as well as his body; that is, by
teaching him to love Jesus Christ. For
this reason you must see that he is properly
instructed; that he prays daily either in
church or in your room; that he goes to

Communion with you on the great Feasts
of the Church. In fact, you must be penetrated with this thought, that he is of the
same flesh and blood as yourself; and that
he is worth a good deal more, if he has
more faith and love.'

Do not let us enter into the little quarrels
they may have with one another, and let
charity prevent our complaining of them
abroad.

If they should be ill, care for them as
a mother. Never let them wait for such
remedies or delicacies as may be ordered
for them.

Above all, *see to them yourself*; do not
delegate this office to others. Console and
exhort them, by motives of faith, to courage and patience. Procure for them such
consolations as their souls may need; and
do not shrink from waiting upon them yourself if necessary, to honour Jesus Christ in
their person, and give their fellow servants
an example of kindness and consideration.

Goodness does not exclude firmness. God
has given us authority; and He wills that

we should use it with moderation, but without weakness. Very often a just reprimand is withheld, from worldly idleness or cowardice.

'All wrong-doing should be noticed, and punished if need be; only, while making the one who has done wrong feel his fault, you may still encourage him, and have a delicate consideration for his self-love, which is more sensitive in proportion to his dependent position. But if it be a question of some vicious habit, some immorality, or some open act of rebellion against authority, no cleverness or merit of other kinds should prevent a speedy and certain dismissal.' (Mdme. de Marcey.)

'Have we not often admired the order, piety, and regularity which reign in certain old families, who unfortunately become rarer every day? In such households, the duty and thought and love of God and of their masters become, as it were, one in the minds of the servants; for there is a complete unity in these two authorities. They know that it is God's will that they should

serve and love their masters; and they
equally know that their masters wish them,
above all, to serve and love God. Now,
such households are, indeed, blessed; for
their guardian angels rain upon both masters and servants the dews of peace and of
the grace of God.' (Mdme. de Marcey.)

TWENTY-SIXTH DAY.

'Women, as well as men, can take part in the battle for God and for His Church.' St. John Chrysostom.

'The perfection of order is to love God more than ourselves.

'To love ourselves for God.

'And our neighbours, not for ourselves, but as ourselves, for the love of God.

'Such ought to be our rule of life; all virtue is contained in it.' (Bossuet.)

The commandment given us by our Lord when He says, ' Love one another, as I have loved you,' does not only refer to our family and to our own household, but generally to every one. We are placed in the midst of the world, and it is our duty to hold intercourse with our fellow creatures, who are indeed our brethren, however much they may differ from us in faith, in feeling, or in diversity of tastes.

It is in the designs of God that those who are really Christians should live in the midst of those who are not. 'The faithful,' writes St. Augustine, 'form in the world a *chosen band*, who, under the banner of Jesus Christ, courageously fight against the maxims opposed to the Gospel.'

We, then, who call ourselves disciples of the Divine Master, have a positive mission to fulfil here below; and it is in this sense that we may with truth use the beautiful words of St. John Chrysostom, when he says that 'women, as well as men, can take part in the battle for God and for His Church.' The first thing that is necessary, in order to be a real apostle, is that we should raise ourselves, by the power of faith, above a world which our Lord has cursed, and which we yet cannot entirely abandon. No longer, it is true, in this country does the world threaten Christians with cruel torments, as in the first centuries of the Church; but it knows how to make people dread its deser-

tion, and even its smiles. Its cruel stings
pierce like daggers into the hearts of those
who still set a certain value on its judgments.

' Go into the world to fulfil the duties of
your position, to satisfy your husband, and
because it is necessary that you should do
so for your children's sake. Go there even
as an innocent recreation; God allows it
you; under certain circumstances it may be
even a positive obligation; but carry with
you the thought and continual realisation
of God's presence.' (Mgr. Mermillod.)

And this faith will also teach us charity;
for an apostolate may be exercised even in
our drawing-rooms, and often in the middle
of the most brilliant fête. We form part of
a large family. We are, all of us, according
to our Lord's beautiful simile, branches of
the same vine, and we owe to one another
help and support. It is not given to us, women, to preach the word of God; but how
many means have we of attracting to His
service souls with whom we happen to come
in contact, and who perhaps might not even

have known us before! We may do much by our words and by our example. Conversation is one of the most efficacious means of enlightening the mind and heart. A philosopher has called it 'the echo of the soul,' and such indeed ought it ever to be.

Let us, then, begin by banishing from it everything which is not truth itself. 'Let us have ever on our lips,' writes the holy St. Francis of Sales, 'words full of sweetness and kindness; let us take care that our manners be pleasing, so that they may attract others, and make them love the spirit which animates us; let us put aside that tone of superiority, which the habit of commanding so easily gives; let us carefully avoid also that patronising spirit, which is so wounding to those whom we consider our inferiors; let us be always willing to praise the good which we see in others, even when it is full of imperfection; and let us disbelieve the evil we hear until publicity or proof makes it certain.'

Who does not prefer a kind-hearted woman to one who is only clever? Let us, then,

strive to be kind and loving. To make religion attractive to all around us is one of the
proofs of real goodness.

'I have often seen religious people attract
wonderfully those who were not so. A life
under the influence of faith, the sweetness
which emanates from it, the interior prism
which throws its light on the outside,—all
this exercises a charm often unknown to
those who are affected by it.' (Mdme. Swetchine.)

'We ought to have that indulgence and
consideration for others which will enable us
to draw out their thoughts and feelings.
Any species of cleverness or learning which
makes us incapable of being kind, obliging,
indulgent, and considerate towards others;
anything which prevents our being easy of
access, or which does not produce in others
the feeling of being pleased both with themselves and with us; in one word, whatever
prevents our being amiable and loving, is a
wrong kind of cleverness.' (Joubert.)

Advice given at a propitious moment, a
few words of encouragement, that kind of

silent disapprobation which arrests detraction, and is often the best way of putting a stop to it—all these are means which assuredly we can each of us use with the greatest advantage, both to our neighbours and to ourselves. Our example may also be to the world, as well as to our own family, a true apostolate. What would not be the power of a certain number of really Christian women, united together in the same wish, that of saving souls, and showing by their conduct that it is possible to be really religious, and at the same time to be sociable and amiable? 'Let strength adorned with grace be your clothing. In church, out of doors, in your homes, let your countenance be the mirror of all that one most loves to fancy as natural in the heart of a good and religious woman; let your smile have a supernatural charm, your looks be a picture of your feelings; let your bearing be stamped with the dignity and simplicity of real religion; and let everything about you command respect, attract others, and raise their standard of character.' (Mgr. Laudriot.)

'Let us endeavour to resemble those women who pass through life like a summer
breeze, vivifying and cheering all who cross
their path.' (Mdme. de Krüdner.)

A Christian woman, who is thoroughly
imbued with the holiness of her mission, will
find in everything a means of fulfilling it.
There are no circumstances, no actions,
however trifling they may appear, which will
not give her an opportunity of preaching our
dear Lord without her intention being sus-
pected.   Is it not in truth to preach it
when we go and visit the worldly and frivolous with the desire of raising, if only for
a moment, their hearts and minds above
the futilities in which they are habitually
absorbed?   Is it not to preach Jesus Christ
when we visit the sick in order to watch, so
to say, for the moment when his soul will
leave this world, that he may be provided
with the consolations of religion, which he
otherwise would perhaps have been deprived
of? Is it not preaching our good God when
we go and visit a friend who is in sorrow, in
the hopes of making her feel the nothing-

ness of the things of this world, and that
our sole happiness consists in serving and
loving God, and His creatures for His sake ?
Do we not preach Jesus Christ when we are
the means of putting a stop to some scan-
dalous conversation, or checking some im-
proper remarks, or when, by the simplicity
and modesty of our own dress, we protest
against a culpable excess of luxury in others,
and still more against the shamelessness of
some women, who, incapable of fascinating
men either by the beauty of their persons or
by the cultivation of their minds, endeavour
to attract observation by pandering to the
worst passions of the human heart ? Is it
not to preach Jesus Christ when we take by
the hand the woman who has lost her own
self-esteem, or when we look with kindness
and tenderness on the weak and the dis-
heartened, whom a little interest on our part
can so greatly cheer? Is it not to preach
Jesus Christ when we show by our words and
actions that we do not belong to ourselves,
but that we have given ourselves up to
others, and are devoted to their good, and

ever ready to help them? Lastly, do we
not preach Jesus Christ when we go into
society for the sake of teaching others un-
consciously how to live in the world and yet
not be of it?' (Mdme. de Marcey.)

We are continually told that we have
great influence over our surroundings; let
us then not neglect it; let us be apostles according to our capabilities and opportunities.
God gives us in these days a large share in
the work of regeneration which all allow to
be so necessary. It is evident that, during
our Lord's sojourn on earth, the Blessed
Virgin and St. Joseph prepared a great
number of souls to receive the all-powerful
grace of salvation. Let us follow their example. 'Courage, then, courage, for our
enemies are but feeble; courage, for God's
work will be accomplished.' (Ozanam.)

'Let us unite ourselves with the Apostles
in their labours and their battles, so that we
may one day have some part in the glory of
their crown.' (St. John Chrysostom.)

TWENTY-SEVENTH DAY.

ON ALMSGIVING.

'The rich and the poor have met one another: the Lord is the maker of them both.' PROVERBS.

OUR Lord has made almsgiving a formal precept, attaching to its fulfilment the promise of magnificent rewards, and threatening with terrible chastisements those who neglect it.

Almsgiving is a general law. If you have much, says Holy Scripture, give much; if you have little, give little; for 'it is the heart which gives to all things their real value.' (St. Ambrose.)

'When the rich man gives an alms, let him not think much of himself, for it is but a debt which he is discharging. It is the legitimate portion of the poor, which he cannot refuse without injustice. True, he

gives honour to God by his alms, but he
honours Him as does the vassal when he
recognises his lord's dominion, and renders
him the obedience which is his due.   He
honours Him as does a faithful steward who
distributes the money which has been intrusted to him, not in his own name, but in
that of his master.

'Pay attention to these words, of which
perhaps you have never yet really taken in
the meaning.   The rich man is the dispen-
ser; but God is the Lord.   The rich man
has the management of the whole house
—he conducts and governs it; but it is
God who created him for that very purpose.
The poor form a part of the great household of God, and there is enough for all the
members of it, only it must be distributed
to all in a just proportion.'   (St. John Chrysostom.)   'We may almost say that in the
divine economy the rich are the elder brothers of the human family, the stewards of
the Father's treasures.'   (Bourdaloue.)   'You
are most guilty,' says St. Ambrose, 'if know-
ingly you allow one of your brethren to

endure hunger.' 'You become the mur-
derer of the poor man whom you do not
relieve.' (St. John Chrysostom.) 'The
superfluity of the rich belongs to the poor;
he who retains it for himself is retaining
that which belongs to others.' (St. Augustine.)

Have we ever reflected that we shall have
to give an account for the neglect of almsgiving, just as much as, for instance, for the
sin of robbery? It must be so, since it is
our bounden duty to help and succour the
poor. 'To know the rights of others; to
fight for them as for our own rights; to
maintain them, even against ourselves when
it is necessary, by crushing in our hearts
our evil inclinations, I mean that selfishness
which loves itself before and in spite of
every one—*that* is to love our neighbour as
ourselves, *that* is justice, not justice in the
abstract, but practical justice.

'How shall we define almsgiving? Surely
for most of you the word almsgiving means
something more than a piece of money
thrown into the hands of a beggar; for you

might in this way get rid of a great deal of
money, without in the eyes of faith fulfilling the law of charity.   The word almsgiving means compassion, love, mercy, and
pity.'   (Gratry.)

Nor can there be any real Christian life
without charity thus understood.

' Religion, clean and undefiled before God
and the Father, is this,' says the Apostle
St. James—' to visit the fathers and the
widows in their tribulation; and to keep
oneself unspotted from this world:' thus
making, it would seem, active charity a
condition for the preservation of purity
amidst the temptations of this life.   ' If we
possessed in our souls that loving pity and
compassion which is so pleasing to God, we
should be able to contemplate the whole
world with that divine and almost maternal
solicitude with which Jesus looked at the
nations of the earth, when, as the Gospel
tells us, He saw them prostrate, smitten
down, and trodden under foot.'   (Gratry.)

Our Divine Legislator speaks to us of the
poor in a manner so forcible that it at first

astonishes us; for He assures us that, whatsoever we do unto the least of His little
ones, it is to Himself that we do it.

'Poverty becomes therefore a sort of
moral personage under which the Godhead
Himself is hidden; for if it is the beggar
who stretches out his hand, it is God Himself who receives the alms.' (St. John
Chrysostom.)

'He becomes security for the poor, and
He repays with usury whatever is lent to
them.' (St. Léon.)

'Almsgiving is a sort of treaty made
with God, and sealed with His seal.' (Ecclus.)

And surely we must see the whole bearing of this divine teaching, and especially
the respect we ought to feel for the poor,
since they are in fact the impersonification
of the Saviour Himself, who made poverty
the companion of His whole life. It was
poverty that received Him, with Mary and
Joseph, in the stable at Bethlehem. It followed Him into Egypt, to Nazareth, and
throughout the long years of His apos-

tolate; again, during the cruel days of His Passion it never left Him ; and it was in the arms of poverty that He expired on the Cross. Therefore is it that Bossuet says : ' If the rich hold the first places in this world, in the kingdom of Jesus Christ it is the poor who are in the foremost ranks. If in this world it is the powerful and the rich who receive favours and privileges, in the Church of Jesus Christ the poor may claim His graces as their right, and it is only from their hands that the rich receive them.'

' When our Lord speaks of the merit of fasting and of virginity, He offers us the kingdom of heaven as a reward; but when it is almsgiving or charity which He is enforcing, or if He tells us to be merciful, then He holds out a far higher prize. What is this prize?   " Ye shall be images of your Father in heaven."' (St. John Chrysostom.)

Again, when He recommends to us the practice of the evangelical counsels, He makes almsgiving the very first condition.

Let us remember the young man in the Gospels. He wished to follow Jesus, assuring Him that he had kept the commandments from his youth upwards, yet the Divine Master said to him: 'Sell what thou hast, and give to the poor, and follow Me.' Thus did He constitute charity the very entrance gate to perfection. Let us not forget that, by almsgiving, we in reality receive far more than we give. 'In exchange for these material things you shall have spiritual riches; and instead of a little money, you will receive the remission of your sins; you save the poor man from hunger, but he will save you from the vengeance of God; you relieve his bodily wants, but it is your own soul that you are really clothing with glory.'

'Your gifts cannot cleanse the poor from the stains of their sins, but your own sins will by them be washed away.' (St. John Chrysostom.)

According to the original and forcible expression of St. Augustine, God, so to say, puts up heaven for sale; He wills that a glass of water should be the price, giving us thereby to understand that 'if you have pity on the poor, even if you have nothing to give them, your very pity is an alms which God accepts.'

Almsgiving is, too, the necessary accompaniment of all real prayer. 'Thy supplications and thy alms,' says the angel to Cornelius, 'are gone up before God, and He has remembered thee.'

'Prayer is a flame of fire, especially when it proceeds from a pious and fervent soul; but the flame requires oil that it may be nourished, and be enabled to rise up to heaven. And this oil, what is it but almsgiving? Pour it out, then, liberally, so that the joy of your good works may stimulate you to pray with more fervour and confidence. We are all of us beggars before God; but in order that God may acknowledge His supplicants, let us not ignore our own. What right have you to ask anything of God, if you refuse to help and relieve your neighbour?'

'True Charity lives ever in the presence

of God, and obtains from Him whatever she asks; Charity breaks the sinner's chains, by chasing away the darkness where they were dwelling, and preserving them from ever-lasting fire. The gates of heaven are ever open to her, and when, like a queen, she makes her entry, no one dare ask her who she is, or whence she comes. For come whence she will, and how she will, she is ever received in triumph. Charity is a virgin, and she has two golden wings, with which she has taken her flight to heaven. Everywhere about her are inscribed these words: "honour and glory." Her loins are girded, her countenance is lovely and gentle, swift and agile is her bearing, and she is ever employed before the throne of God in dispensing His treasures.' (St. John Chrysostom.)

TWENTY-EIGHTH DAY.

ON ALMSGIVING (*continued*).

'Not in bread alone doth man live, but in every word that proceedeth from the mouth of God.'

THE soul of man is infinitely more precious in the sight of God than the ' *earthly taber-nacle*' in which it is enveloped, and which day by day is tending to decay; for this reason is it that spiritual alms have a far greater merit in the sight of God than mere corporal charities.

We are assured by statistics, the accuracy of which we should be glad to test, that in rich and beautiful France more than 50,000 die every year in consequence of the privations which poverty imposes on them. Is not this a heavy responsibility for the upper classes of society? And then, who can ever tell the prodigious number of souls who perish from the results of ignorance and prejudice? What a vast field for our own zeal! and how blest should we be, both by God and men, were we seriously to undertake a crusade against so many and combined evils! Let us, then, have a real and courageous love of our brethren; especially let us love their souls, not only for their moral grandeur, but for that which is holiest and most sacred in them.

Let us give them not only the fervour of an ever-growing charity, but that entire devotedness, that absolute gift of ourselves, and that resolution of purpose, which inspires certain noble souls to consecrate their whole lives, their fortune, and their labour, to the religious and moral improvement of their fellow-men.

'There are two distinct kinds of men on the earth; those who injure souls, and those who do them good. These two divisions of men are equally zealous and powerful in the world.

'They are separate in everything, and are

as antagonistic to each other as God and the
devil.   One set, with audacious and daring
frenzy, suggest to every soul they come near
falsehood, scandal, treachery, dishonour, and
despair. This is their greatest delight. The
other, on the contrary, inspire souls with
respect, love, truth, the enjoyment of all
that is pure and good, holy affections, honour, courage in this life, and hope in heaven.
And they also find joy in their work, and
only live for its accomplishment.' (L'Abbé
Perreyre.)

'Do you know the price of a soul?   Do
you know what value is set by God and His
angels on that poor man of whom you think
so little?   Do you see in him the Christ
who has redeemed you?   If you do, then
will you too go forth in search of His lambs,
and of the sheep who have gone astray.
And your charity will first show itself in
respect, because the object of your charity is
indeed worthy of all honour; and then in
tenderness, because the first want of the
poor is what the heart alone can give, inasmuch as their hearts are often more in want

of kindness than of bread. And then you will be charitable towards the souls of the poor; for if it be true, that it is a noble action to go to the poor man's house in order to teach him the science of life, to revive his courage, provide him with work, and to restore his self-respect and independence, it surely is a far better action to awake sleeping souls, to rouse them from their ignorance, and to speak to them of eternal truths and hopes; for then the benefit we have conferred no longer resembles the stone thrown into an abyss, which for a second makes a deep sound, and then remains silent and immovable.' (L'Abbé Baunard.)

Has it not often happened to us, when we have met with cases of especial distress, to regret that we were not the possessors of some great treasure? Have we not often exclaimed, 'If I were but richer!' But in fulfilling the great duty of spiritual charity we never can feel this difficulty; for the wealth we have to dispense is endless, God being its everlasting source. Our part, therefore, should be to draw out of the Heart of our Divine Master some of His priceless graces, and then go and distribute them amongst the poor. I have seen weak and feeble women kneel day after day at the Lord's table, their souls thereby being kindled with fresh fervour. And when they had partaken of the sacred Banquet, they hastened, like the Apostles of old, to the dwellings of the poor, to bear to them the glad tidings of salvation. Such women might, indeed, repeat with the Apostle, 'It is no longer I who live, it is Jesus Christ who lives in me.' It is our Divine Lord, who by their lips teaches and consoles the sufferers, so that they might well say, when their visitors had left them, to continue elsewhere their apostolic work, 'Was not our heart burning within us whilst He spoke?' (St. Luke xxiv. 22.)

O, did we but compare the good thus accomplished with all that the cold philanthropy of the world can effect, we should indeed feel that there is a deep abyss between the one and the other.

' O, how beautiful are the feet of that
apostolic woman ! How beautiful and touching are the words which fall from her lips !
How rich and abundant are the harvests
she is preparing ! Harvests of peace, of
calmness, of strength, of courage, and of
love !' (Mgr. Laudriot.)

A heart, filled with the burning desire of
spreading in the world that divine fire which
our Lord came down from heaven to kindle,
will not be content with words of consolation, advice, or encouragement. By fervent
and continual prayer she will draw down a
blessing on her work. How many souls
will be saved by such humble supplications !

Let us adopt the pious custom of some
women, who never pass by one of our Lord's
poor without drawing down upon him by
their prayers the blessing of God. Alas, it
is not only the poor in the goods of this
world whom we ought to help in this manner; but perhaps even our relations or our
friends, who, although rich in earthly posses-
sions, are yet destitute and miserable in the
sight of God.

The power of intercession is a deposit placed in our hands by God, just as much as material riches. Both are among the talents of which the Gospel speaks, and of which we shall have to give an account. Were we to pray more, these souls which we love, and whose indifference for everything that regards God we deplore, might through His infinite mercy have a hope of salvation.

What a torrent of blessings and of grace poured forth, nineteen centuries ago, from that humble Nazareth home, where Jesus, Mary, and Joseph addressed to Almighty God such fervent prayers for the salvation of souls. A pious tradition tells us, that in spite of their own poverty, they still found enough wherewith to help their neighbours. But what comparison was there between the material alms they bestowed, and the inestimable treasures which were the fruits of their intercession?

We have other brethren whose hands are raised in prayer towards us, whilst their heart-rending supplications ring in our ears. "Have pity on me, have pity on me, at least

you my friends, because the hand of the
Lord hath touched me.' (Job.)

God, by an impenetrable mystery, has, as
it were, tied His hands with respect to the
satisfaction which is due to His justice from
the souls in Purgatory; but at the same
time He has placed in our own the price
of their ransom; and 'what, indeed, can be
more soothing to our hearts than this pious
devotion, which unites us to the memory
and to the sufferings of our dear departed
ones?   Belief in the efficacy of prayer and
good deeds for the relief of those whom
we have lost; the belief, that when we
mourn for them, our tears may help them;
the belief, in a word, that even in the invisible world which they inhabit, our love
may still be of use to them,—is not this a
sweet and blessed belief? and what consolation does it not contain for those who have
seen death enter their homes and knock at
the very door of their hearts? This mixture
of religion and sorrow, of prayer and love,
has in itself something exquisitely touching
and beautiful: never, indeed, do faith, hope,

and charity better meet together to honour
God, whilst they give comfort to men ; and
thus does the relief of the dead become the
consolation of the living.' (Le P. Félix.)

How much might not still be said upon
this vast subject of charity towards our
brethren !

There will come a day when God will demand of us an exact account of our adminis-
tration, in that great court of assize, of
which He Himself gives us a description.
It would seem as if He would judge His
creatures almost entirely by the beautiful
law of charity. Listen to Him dividing the
multitude into two parts, and saying to
them, 'Come, ye blessed of My Father.'
He will say to the elect, ' For I was hungry, and you gave Me to eat; I was thirsty,
and you gave Me to drink; I was naked,
and you clothed Me; I was sick, and you
visited Me.' And to the lost He will say,
'Depart from Me, ye cursed; for I was
hungry, and ye gave Me not to eat; I was
thirsty, and you gave Me not to drink; I
was sick, and you did not visit Me.'

O, may this awful scene, of which at the end of the world we shall ourselves be the witnesses, give food to our most serious reflections !

TWENTY-NINTH DAY.

THE LAST AGONY.

'My Father, if it be possible, let this chalice pass from Me; nevertheless not as I will, but as Thou wilt.' ST. MATT. xxvi. 42.

IN spite of the revolt of our nature, we are obliged to acknowledge that life has only been given to us in order that by penance and by suffering we may gain heaven; both are the inheritance left by guilty man to his posterity. We all of us suffer; nothing can exempt us from this common law, which affects alike the child in its cradle, the old man on his death-bed, the poor in their misery, and the king on his throne. The law of sacrifice is the fundamental law of Christian life, and every soul who desires to belong to God must fulfil it. There is nothing great in the world without sacrifice and the cross.

Suffering is expiation; suffering is merit; suffering is love. And we may say that every day of our lives is, so to say, stamped with the seal of suffering, until that day when God, the Sovereign Lord of life and death, will break the bonds which unite our souls to our body. But, since man was not created to die, and that death is but the consequence of sin, when the solemn moment of separation comes, there is ever a final struggle between the two different parts of which we are composed. The agony of death is the revolt of nature at the approaching dissolution of the body.

But let us for a moment leave this last agony, of which we shall speak again in our meditation on death itself; and let us hear what the Gospel tells us about another agony, which might be called ' the agony of the soul,'—the agony of our Saviour.

After the institution of the Holy Eucharist, Jesus withdrew into the garden with His Apostles, and said to them : ' My soul is sorrowful even unto death.' (St. Matt. xxvi. 38.) ' And He withdrew from them a stone's

cast; and kneeling down He prayed, saying,
Father, if Thou wilt, remove this chalice
from Me. But yet not My will but Thine
be done.' 'And there appeared to Him an
angel from heaven strengthening Him; and
being in an agony He prayed the longer,
and His sweat became as drops of blood
trickling down upon the ground.' (St. Luke
xxii. 41.)

We have, all of us, in our lives experienced some hour, some moment, which
corresponds with the agony of our Divine
Lord; that terrible hour when sorrow has
reached its height, when the cup of suffering
is presented to us by the angel of the Lord;
and in the midst of our groans, and in the
excess of our misery, we exclaim, ' My God,
this is more than I can bear!'

It is the sword of sacrifice; but it presents itself to each one of us under a different
aspect. To Abraham, it was the command
to sacrifice his only son; to Jacob, the news
of Joseph's death; to Job, his complete de-
sertion by all; to David, the treachery and
death of Absolom; to the mother of the

Macchabees, the sevenfold martyrdom of her
beloved children; to Joseph, the loss of our
Saviour in the Temple; to Mary, the cruci-
fixion of her Son: that was the terrible hour
when, standing at the foot of the cross, she
cried out in her anguish: 'O, all ye who
pass by, look and see whether there is any
sorrow like unto my sorrow.'

Model mother as she was, she underwent
a martyrdom more agonising than a thousand
deaths, for it was in her arms that the dead
body of her Child was laid.

And what for us will be this trial of trials,
this most terrible of all crosses? O, if the
dreaded hour is not yet come, too well shall
we know it by the piercing of our heart, by
the anguish of our soul!

The tide of sorrow will rise higher and
higher; desolation will take possession of us;
and, like Jesús in the garden of Olives, we
shall feel ourselves alone and abandoned; no
one will be there to save or to help us, and
trembling and forsaken, we shall not know
where to hide ourselves, for God Himself will
appear deaf to our cries. We are already in

the dark and narrow passage, of which Bossuet speaks; we must go through it, *we
must;* but nature resists and draws back,
and then it is that we feel the crushing
weight of moral agony; our soul is sorrowful even unto death, and we turn away our
head, saying, 'Lord, Lord, let this chalice
be taken away from me!' And we push it
back. 'Rather will we die,' do we exclaim,
in the excess of our anguish. But God has
spoken, and it must be borne. That life,
which was a million times dearer to us than
our own, has run its course; the decree of
death has gone forth, and no power can stay
the Divine Hand; or, we trusted in affection, in natural gratitude; and suddenly we
find ourselves the victims of the basest ingratitude and treachery. Our most legitimate
hopes are cruelly disappointed; our best-
conceived plans are disconcerted.

But, whether it be the death of those dear
to us, or treachery, or deception, or ruin, it
always is the two-edged sword of which the
Scriptures speak; the wound it makes in our
hearts is so deep, that it can never be healed;

and our tears—the blood of our souls—will flow until our last hour.

Yet all the while God is near to us, though we feel it not. Although He hides Himself from us, He does not abandon His children; He makes us pass through this time of misery as gold passes through the crucible; for trials and sorrows are to our souls what the storm is to the pilot, the fight to the athlete, or the battle to the soldier. We are so knocked down that we think all is lost, and that we are left without hope; but we cannot perish, for He is with us in whose hands are life and death. Jesus, our model and our Saviour, deigned to undergo His cruel agony, in order that His anguish, and the precious Blood which dropped from Him in the excess of His suffering, should merit for us the great grace of resignation, that wonderful gift by which we seem to place God between ourselves and our grief. And, after all, can there be one moment in our existence, even the darkest, when it is not our duty to say with our Blessed Lord, Thy will be done, and not mine! Let us

never forget, that before the eternal heights
can be reached, man, as the poet has beauti-
fully said, must pass through 'the weeping
fields;' and that, as the royal Prophet tells
us, if we 'sow in tears' in the furrows of this
life, the day will come when, through the
mercy of God, we shall 'reap in joy.'

THIRTIETH DAY.

ON DEATH.

'The just need patience to bear their lives; and find delight in death.' St. Augustine.

' Lift up your eyes to heaven, and amidst all its brilliant constellations, look and see if there be one which can reveal to you the secret of your salvation, or which shall point out to you what God would do to purify, regenerate, and draw all souls to Himself. Alas, I, who know the secret, hesitate to tell it to you; so vulgar, and yet so deep; so wondrous, and yet so commonplace, is it. How often have you seen without comprehending it, this sovereign and incomprehensible thing, which redeems the world, which is at the same time the sword of justice, the smile of love, and the choice of a heart fixed on God. Bow your head and hear the word : It is death !' (Le Père Lacordaire.)

Death is, in truth, a punishment and a deliverance. Created for immortality, man was destined to pass, without a shock, from the delights of the Garden of Eden to the full possession of God; but with sin, death —which was its punishment— came into the world. It must have been something very terrible which God awarded as a punishment for the fault of Adam and Eve. Perhaps they did not understand, at first, the full bearing of the divine sentence; but death appeared to them in all its terrors when the first blow was struck, and when, having left Abel young, beautiful, and full of life, they only found his bloody and disfigured remains.

In the beginning of the world, this mother weeping over the inanimate body of her son reveals to us all the horror and agony which accompanies death. But let us cast our eyes on another mother, whom God has struck in the person of her Son. It is death, still, with its agony and its sorrow; but it is also life; for He who was nailed to the Cross, and who shed on guilty humanity even to the last drop of His Blood, is about to roll away the stone of the sepulchre and rise again in glory. He will be the first-born among the dead who can exclaim, ' O death! where is thy sting ? O death ! where is thy victory ?' His resurrection is the pledge of our own. For those who are His children there is no more death ; for ' the souls of the just are in the hand of God, and the fear of death will not reach them.' Nevertheless, the Word of God is eternal and immutable. Man must die. We must every one of us pass through the narrow portals of the tomb; but in His infinite mercy the Saviour, by accepting death, took away all its bitterness ; so that to the Christian to die is to live.

The inferior part of ourselves will perhaps experience some terrors at the approach of death ; but the soul, soaring above the material world, may exclaim with the Prophet: ' I rejoiced when it was said to me, We will go into the house of my Father.'

St. Augustine's words, which we have quoted in the beginning of this meditation, are true; as to the saints, death is only a passage to the fruition of a higher love.

'I weary, O my God,' he writes, 'of this painful pilgrimage called life; of this miserable existence, subject to so many thousand ills capable at any moment of destroying it. Everything here below is uncertain, except the troubles and sorrows we shall meet with on our road. All around us we see sin and wrongdoing; the wicked are masters of the situation, the proud triumph, and we are exposed to so many falls and miseries that it is less life than death. What, after all, is this existence of ours, where prosperity inflates us, and adversity casts us down; where youth is full of temerity and inconstancy, and old age is nothing but heaviness and torpor; where a thousand ills and infirmities oppress us, and a thousand sorrows weigh us down with misery!'

For all of us, in fact, life has many bitter days; and the more we advance in our career, the more we feel that we are not made for the treacherous joys of this world. 'Death,' writes the Père Lacordaire, 'by recalling the soul to God and the body to earth, accomplishes a wonderful deliverance in our favour. It sows in us the germ of a new and stainless birth in the resurrection. We must be born again a second time. Our Lord, therefore, will only untie the threads of our existence, while from the shadows of the grave will come forth the light which will lighten all the human race.'

This is what St. Augustine has also so admirably expressed : ' One thing only have I asked of God, which I shall ever persist in— that I may live in His house all the days of my life. As the hart panteth for the water-brook, so panteth my soul for Thee, O my God ! When shall I appear before the presence of God? When shall I see Him for whom my soul thirsteth? When shall I see Him in the land of the living? for in this Valley of Death my eyes see Him not. What shall I do, miserable man that I am, fast bound and tied in the bands of this mortal life? What shall I do? As long as we are in the body we are absent from the

we seek one to come. It is in heaven—in
heaven alone—that we shall find our real inheritance.   Must I for ever stretch out my
arms towards Thee without ever reaching
Thee? without ever being able to embrace
Thee, to lose myself in Thee by dying entirely to myself?   O love! O dying to self!
O attaining at last unto the beatific vision
of God!   Alas, how long our exile seems!
I have lived among the tents of Kedar; but
O, how strange is my soul in the midst of
them!   Who will give me the wings of a
dove, that I may fly away, and be at rest
for ever?' (St. Augustine.)

Let us listen to the pious aspirations of a
truly Christian soul.

'A rapid decline, a strong impetus, draws
me towards the grave; every hour strips
me of something fresh and hastens the
end.   The grains of sand at the top of my
hour-glass are fewer and fewer, and I count
them without fear.   How solemn are the
years which remain to us — those years
which may be cut short in a single day!
The eve of each anniversary brings with it

a graver character ; for we know not if the dawn may not rise on eternity.

' *Nunc dimittis !* Now, O God, let Thy servant depart in peace. Her earthly burdens are so lightened, that the weakest of Thine angels might bear her on his wings. Her pride is humbled ; *le moi* has lost its importance ; the world has withdrawn its favours ; the weight of sin has been removed by contrition, by tears, by absolution ; and under Thine easy yoke her neck is bent in submission, in patience, in resignation. At last the day is come for which we were born ; this day, in view of which alone we ought to have lived ; this day so dreaded, yet so longed for ; this day, which rises as the star of our eternal destiny ; this hour— " this is the day which the Lord hath made ;" for to us the resurrection means death, in the first instance. On the threshold of two worlds the spouse pauses and trembles before she springs forward into His everlasting arms. O my God ! acknowledge her as Thine own, by the sacred sign on her forehead ; by the lamp which she bears in her hands; by the ardent flame which Thou hast enkindled in her heart! Own her as Thine; stretch out Thine hand to save her; call her by her name; grant that she may hear Thy voice and answer it!

'May everything in us, O my God, hasten to bow before Thy supreme decree! May the mortification of our senses and of self have emptied our hearts of all but Thee, before the earthly thread of our life be severed! O God, grant that I may leave this world disengaged from all worldly ties, purified in soul and spirit, free from doubts and terrors, poor, simple, little, like one of the children whom Thou hast blessed! Deign to cast upon me a look of love and compassion, which may prepare me for this terrible passage. And may the pardon of my sins have preceded me before Thy judgment-seat!' (Mdme. Swetchine.)

And how can we fear, besides, we, who honour with a special devotion him who had the singular grace of being permitted to yield his soul into the hands of God in the arms of Jesus; and who was sustained likewise by the fervent prayers of Mary! Let us invoke him each day, so that our last moments of agony and struggle may be full of inward calm, and that we may sleep in peace in tho heart of our Lord. For to the true Christian death is but a sleep, of which the awakening is in heaven.

THIRTY-FIRST DAY.

ON HEAVEN.

'If you fear the toil, let the thought of the reward encourage you.' St. Augustine.

God wills that man's perfection should consist in the accomplishment of His laws. We began by stating that it is His will that we should be just towards all; that is, that we should render to every one his due. But, at the same time, He has made solemn promises to man, that the fulfilment of duty shall bring with it its reward. 'Well done, good and faithful servant! Because thou hast been faithful over a few things, I will place thee over many things; enter thou into the joy of thy Lord.'

But God is infinite goodness. And this price of our work, these wages for our toil, will infinitely surpass our labours or our pains. 'The sufferings of the present time are not worthy to be compared with the glory which shall be revealed in us,' writes the Apostle. But how can we speak of a happiness which our feeble minds cannot even understand? The Apostle was ravished to the third heaven, and confesses himself unable to describe to us the marvels of which he was for a few moments the eye-witness.

'The eye hath not seen, O God, besides Thee, what things Thou hast prepared for them that wait for Thee.' (Isaiah lxiv. 4.) If, in the midst of the many and varied trials of this life, we place all our confidence in God, then heaven appears to us as the end of all our sorrows. To the weary and suffering, death is a sweet rest; to the poor mariner, tossed for a long while on the waves of this troublesome world, heaven is the port which he is striving to attain. To the captive, it is liberty; to the exile, it is home; to the soldier, it is victory; to the broken heart, it is love and peace and consolation. And besides all that, it is eternal happiness; for God Himself will be in the midst of the souls whom

He has ransomed. We find in the Holy
Scriptures endless references to the ineffable
joys which God has prepared for us; of
which we will only select one or two:

'Behold, I create new heavens and a new
earth; and the former things shall not be
in remembrance, and they shall not come
upon the heart. But you shall be glad,
and rejoice for ever in these things which
I create; for, behold, I create Jerusalem a
rejoicing, and the people thereof joy. And
I will rejoice in Jerusalem and joy in My
people, and the voice of weeping shall no
more be heard in her, nor the voice of cry-
ing.' (Isaiah lxv. 17, 18, 19.)   'And they
that are redeemed by the Lord shall return
and shall come into Sion, singing praises;
and joy everlasting shall be upon their
heads; they shall obtain joy and gladness,
and sorrow and mourning shall flee away.'
(Isaiah li. 11.)

'Jerusalem, abode of ineffable peace!   O,
city of God, Holy Zion, our own true country, what a torrent of consolations wilt
thou pour into the souls that look for thee !

Who shall measure the illimitable riches of Christ's Kingdom? There shall we behold the King of our hearts in all the splendour of His Divinity. There shall the elect be fed with celestial food, whilst they contemplate in ecstasy the beauty of their Spouse. There the angelic choirs unite in singing harmonies unknown to human ears.' (St. Laurence Justinian.)

'O heavenly country, vast and fertile land, containing all we most love! O divine city, what glorious things are spoken of thee, thou city of God! Thou art the abode of all those who enjoy the Beatific Vision; who behold the Lamb of God seated on His throne in all His beauty and glory; who hear His sweet and penetrating voice. O, how sweet it is to love and to possess God! He alone suffices us. Without Him we are lost; with Him and in Him are all things. We can never weary of His presence, we can never love Him enough; in Him is life and happiness; our minds revel in His truth; and love is renewed every instant in presence of infinite and uncreated beauty.

'O happy vision, to see God in His essence and behold Him in His glory. All that we could possibly dream of or desire we shall then possess, and our souls will be abundantly satisfied. God will be known and loved, the mind and heart will be filled to overflowing, and man's beatitude will be consummated.

'The Blessed Virgin, when she was translated into heaven, added to the joy of its inhabitants. What will be the delight of those whom she has protected here below, and who have so often experienced the benefit of her powerful intercession, when they shall at last hear her soft voice, contemplate her wonderful countenance, and enjoy her holy presence? Mary, whose virginal purity shines with redoubled splendour in the heavenly court!' (St. Bernard.)

St. Joseph is there, as at Bethlehem, between Jesus and Mary. And He whose infant steps he was privileged to guide has given him great powers. Can Jesus, who deigned to be subject to him for thirty years, refuse anything to the prayers of this glorious Patriarch? How many souls, O great Saint, will perhaps owe to thee their entrance into the heavenly country?

But the last solemn hour for us has not yet struck: we are still pilgrims and sojourners in this vale of tears. Ah, may we at last comprehend the utter nothingness of all that now troubles and absorbs us here below, repeating often that beautiful prayer of St. Augustine:

'My soul has glimpses now and then of a ray of Thy glory, which already fills her with joy. Ah, Lord, if this light were increased, if Thy beauty were revealed to my feeble sight, would my being be able to bear such delights without dissolution? It is Thine to grant me what Thou wilt. All I ask is that Thou wilt make me capable of receiving greater light and deeper love. For even with the little spark vouchsafed to us in this world, I feel my whole soul set on fire. What, then, would it be if it were given me to contemplate Thee in all the splendour of Thy glory? May the hour come quickly when, filled with ineffable

and celestial joy, I may exclaim : I behold
Thee, then, Thou whom I have so ardently
desired! I hold Thee, in whom I have
hoped; I possess Thee, for whom I have
longed; I am united to Thee whom I have
so deeply loved. It is Thou whom I praise,
whom I bless, whom I adore; Thou, my
God, who liveth and reigneth for ever and
ever, and in all ages. Amen.'

In conclusion, I love to rest in the promise given by St. Theresa to her spiritual
daughters : 'All the graces you may ask of
God, through the intercession of St. Joseph,
will be granted to you, for I have never
invoked him in vain.'

May this great protector of those souls
who wish to live in union with Jesus and
Mary be with them in life and death ! May he
listen to my prayer, and cause these few poor
lines that I have written to be useful to
some of my sisters in the faith, and then
my most ardent wish will be realised.

PRAYERS IN HONOUR OF ST. JOSEPH.

LITANY OF THE HOLY HEART OF ST. JOSEPH.

Lord, have mercy on us.

Jesus Christ, have mercy on us.

Lord, have mercy on us.

Jesus Christ, hear us.

Jesus Christ, graciously hear us.

God the Father of heaven,

God the Son, Redeemer of the world,

God the Holy Ghost,

Holy Trinity, one God,

Heart of Jesus, source of all grace,

Heart of Mary, conceived without sin,

Heart of Joseph, filled with the gifts of the Holy Ghost,

Heart of Joseph, destined by God to be united to the immaculate heart of Mary,

Have mercy on us.

Pray for us.

Heart of Joseph, overflowing with holy
joy when adoring for the first time the
Child Jesus,

Heart of Joseph, who consoled the heart
of Mary for the hardness of heart of
the inhabitants of Bethlehem,

Heart of Joseph, where the Sacred Heart
of Jesus so often reposed,

Heart of Joseph, instructed by the Heart
of Jesus in all the treasures of grace it
contained,

Heart of Joseph, filled by the Heart of
Jesus with all the gifts of heaven,

Heart of Joseph, so touched by the angels'
song which the shepherds repeated at
the foot of the crib,

Heart of Joseph, who greeted so humbly
the arrival of the three kings,

Heart of Joseph, who didst also present
to Jesus the gold of your faith, the incense of your charity, and the myrrh
of your sorrows,

Heart of Joseph, whose more than paternal kindness was the admiration of the
wise men,

Pray for us.

Heart of Joseph, so resigned at the prospect of the sorrow which holy Simeon foretold for Mary,

Heart of Joseph, sweet hope of the dying,

Heart of Joseph, special protector of St. Theresa, and refuge of all her children,

Lamb of God, who didst find in the heart of Joseph a true father's heart, forgive us our sins.

Lamb of God, who rested from Thy labours on the heart of Joseph, hear our prayers.

Lamb of God, who didst receive the last sigh of the heart of Joseph, have mercy on us, now and at the hour of our death.

Pray for us, O pitiful heart of Joseph, so that we may be ever worthy of thy fatherly protection.

Pray for us.

Prayer.

O, most tender heart of the glorious St. Joseph, we beseech thee to accept the filial homage of our hearts, and ever to reign over them. Obtain for us from our Saviour all the grace necessary to support with patience the troubles of this life, and to advance steadily towards our heavenly home, where we hope to thank and bless thee to all eternity. Amen.

———

PRAYER IN HONOUR OF ST. JOSEPH.
COMPOSED BY ST. THERESA.

Omnipotent and all-merciful Lord, who didst give to the Virgin Mary, Thy most holy Mother, the blessed Joseph, the son of David, as her spouse, and didst choose him for Thy foster-father, grant to Thy Church, through the prayers and by the merits of this great Saint, peace and tranquillity; and give us the grace and the joy of one day seeing Thee eternally in heaven, who livest and reignest with God the Father, in the unity of the Holy Spirit, for ever and ever. Amen.

———

MEMORARE TO ST. JOSEPH.

Remember, O blessed and pitiful Joseph, that never was it known, that any one who fled to thy protection, implored thy help, and sought thy intercession, was left unaided. Inspired with this confidence, I fly unto thee, O holy spouse of the Queen of virgins, my father. To thee I come, before thee I stand, sinful and sorrowful. O foster-father of Jesus, despise not my petitions, but in thy mercy hear and answer me. Amen.

LITTLE OFFICE OF ST. JOSEPH.*

MATINS.

Hail, glory of Patriarchs, steward of God's holy Church!

Thou, who didst preserve and cherish the living Bread, the Corn of the elect.

Lord, open Thou my lips,

And my mouth shall show forth Thy praise.

O God, come to my assistance;

O Lord, make haste to help me.

Glory be to the Father, &c.

Hymn.

Just man, of David's royal line,
God did thee predestinate

* This Office is very ancient, and great graces have been obtained by its recital.

Foster-father of our Lord,
　　Spouse of maid inviolate.
Thou, the servant true and faithful,
　　Head of Nazareth's blest home,
May thy sweet paternal pity
　　On our prayers in blessing come !

Antiphon.

God has established him in His dwelling-place, and has given him dominion over His kingdom.

Pray for us, blessed Joseph, that we may be made worthy of the promises of Jesus Christ.

Prayer.

Grant, O Lord, that we may find in the blessed Spouse of Thy holy Mother, all the help of which we stand in need, so that through his powerful intercession we may receive what we could not by ourselves obtain. We beg this of Thee, O Lord Jesus Christ, who livest and reignest with the Father and the Holy Spirit for ever and ever. Amen.

PRIME.

Hail, glory of Patriarchs.
O God, come to my assistance, &c.
Glory be to the Father, &c.

Hymn.

When thy righteous heart was troubled
 By the mystery divine
Of the Godhead lying hidden
 In the holy virgin shrine,
In a dream the heavenly angel
 Hush'd thy anxious care to rest;
Let our sorrows turn to gladness,
 At God's merciful behest.

Antiphon.

Joseph, son of David, fear not to take
unto thee Mary, thy wife, for that which is
conceived in her is of the Holy Ghost.
Pray for us, blessed Joseph, &c.
And the Prayer, as at Matins.

TIERCE.

Hail, glory of Patriarchs, &c.
O God, come to my assistance, &c.
Glory be to the Father, &c.

Hymn.

Soon shall Bethlehem hail the birthday
  Of the Word for us made flesh ;
Joseph, thou shalt taste the fountain
  Which shall soon the world refresh.
Humbly worshipp'd in the manger,
  Cradled with the undefiled,
Now in highest heaven exalted
  Let us seek the holy Child.

Antiphon.

Joseph also went up from Galilee, out of
the city of Nazareth, into Judea, to the city
of David, which is called Bethlehem, to be
enrolled with Mary, his espoused wife, who
was with child.

Pray for us, &c. (as at Matins).

SEXT.

Hail, glory of Patriarchs, &c.
O God, come to my assistance.
Glory be to the Father, &c.

Hymn.

Vainly shall the cruel Herod
  Seek on Him to lay his hand,

Jesu's angel safe shall guide thee
    Into Egypt's sheltering land;
Thither tremblingly thou fliest
    With the Babe on Mary's breast;
In my hour of fear and peril
    Let my weakness on Him rest.

Antiphon.

Arise, take the Child and His Mother,
and fly into Egypt, and be there until I shall
tell thee. For it will come to pass that
Herod will seek the Child to destroy Him.
Pray for us, &c. (as at Matins).

NONE.

Hail, glory of Patriarchs, &c.
O God, come to my assistance.
Glory be to the Father, &c.

Hymn.

Thou didst worship in the manger
    Him who gently on thee smiled;
He is now in heaven exalted—
    Pray for us to thine own Child.

Antiphon.

Joseph arose, and took the Child and His

Mother, and came into the land of Israel, and coming he dwelt in a city called Nazareth.

Pray for us, &c. (as at Matins).

VESPERS.

Hail, glory of Patriarchs, &c.
O God, come to my assistance, &c.
Glory be to the Father, &c.

Hymn.

Herod dies; the angel calls thee,
  For his death brings thee release;
Past the days of weary exile,
  Find in Nazareth thy peace.
There thy fostering tender care
  Jesu's soft caress returns;
Make thy virtues in us flourish,
  Faith and hope within us burns.

Antiphon.

My Son, why hast Thou done so to us? Behold, Thy father and I have sought Thee sorrowing.

Pray for us, &c. (as at Matins).

COMPLINE.

Hail, glory of Patriarchs, &c.

Convert us, O God our Saviour,
And turn away Thine anger from us.
O God, come to my assistance;
O Lord, make haste to help me.
Glory be to the Father, &c.

Hymn.

O, how bitter was the anguish
    When three days ye sought around,
Till, His Father's business heeding,
    In the Temple He was found!
Sweet was sorrow's soft remonstrance,
    Sweet His words to Mary's heart;
For us, Joseph, interceding,
    May we ne'er from Jesu part.

Antiphon.

I will sleep in peace and I will rest; for
Thou, O Lord, alone hast established me in
hope.

Pray for us, blessed Joseph, that we may
be made worthy of the promises of Jesus
Christ.

Prayer.

Grant, O Lord, that in the blessed Spouse
of Thy holy Mother we may find all the

help of which we stand in need, so that through his powerful intercession we may receive what we could not by ourselves obtain. We beg this of Thee, O Lord Jesus Christ, who livest and reignest with the Father and the Holy Spirit for ever and ever. Amen.

Commendation.

Joseph, thus the charge fulfilling
  Given thee by the Holy One,
Hear a heart that loves thee telling
  What for Jesus thou hast done.
Saint and Patron of the dying,
  Thee I invoke on bended knee,
That God at last my soul requiring,
  May grant me then a place by thee.

THE END.

LONDON:
RODSON AND SONS, PRINTERS, PANCRAS ROAD, N.W.

www.ingramcontent.com/pod-product-compliance
Lightning Source LLC
Chambersburg PA
CBHW030630030726
47497CB00006B/1726